HAMMER TIME

Acknowledgements:

First, I would like to Thank my father... Mr. Curtis Bell Sr., for putting up with all of my bad decision making throughout the long years of me knowing better. And for ALWAYS having my back, and staying down, through all the confusion! I love you pops! To my only two wonderful and beautiful daughters! Zy'Asia & A'Myyah. Through all your hurt and tears... you were not alone! Zy'Asia... words could never express the love that I have for you, nor define how much you mean to me! I've made plenty of bad choices in life, but when I made you... I knew that I would forever have reason to smile. You gave me strength when I had none... and the courage to face the reality of being a father. I lacked precious moments in your life, that you may never forgive me for... due to my incarceration! Thus I want you to know and understand... no matter how far the distance, or miles apart we are. You are... and will always be my flesh and blood! You are my first born... and I understand your hurt and frustrations! You are my daughter! DON'T ever get it confused! I love you and I miss you! "Zy-Zy"... Love Always Dad! A'Myyah... I love you more than you will ever know! There's no perfect words to express how much you mean to me! I apologize to you and your sister for being careless. My own stupidity caused me to miss out, on some of the greatest moments in your life. How can I ever began to repair what was damaged, if I never expressed what mattered the most? And that's seeing you smile, knowing that your happy, healthy and strong! Well as you knowing that your deeply loved and cared about more than you will ever know! You are my youngest daughter, my second born... and I know that things haven't been great between us! But believe me...you! Everyone knows how much I love you, how much you mean to me, and just how beautiful you are! Whether I tell you or not... I ALWAYS brag about you, and your sister! "FACTZ!" I often find myself smiling when I think about our feuds. It's nothing other than a heated moment, of neither one of us wanting to listen and hear each other out! Dammmnnn!! Your attitude is just like mine... but I wouldn't have you no other way! You're my reason for smiling! And ALWAYS know...that my life is incomplete without you! The truth of the matter is... can't nothing ever change the fact that you are my daughter! Don't ever let nothing deceive you. I love you and I miss you... so much! "Myyah." Love Always Dad! To my three beautiful granddaughters...Londyn, Milan, and Mia. I love you sweethearts with all my life and soul! I remember the world would laugh at me... now I'm doing the laughing. Pa Pa... is going to make a way for you'll. BELIEVE IT!! To All 7 of my wonderful sisters, Pudding, Todda, Schrise, Anne, Jennifer, Sharon, and Alexandria. I deal with all of you different, but I forever love all of you equally! Pudding, you're my oldest sister... and my greatest inspiration! You ALWAYS stayed true, no matter what it was that I did, or got into. You would show a n%##@ tuff love, but you never turned your back on me, or forgot about me! And I love you unconditionally for being the wonderful big sister, and person that you are! I wouldn't change you for nothing in the world my love! You know...as I was finishing my book! I thought about you and years ago, when you lived on Lord Ave., and you sent me to Shop rite to buy some ice cream, for the birthday cake... and I bought back some Sorbet! I clearly remember you saying, "Stain... nobody eats Sorbet ice cream with levels that was manifested, A alike attract... unalike repel. Builder's always build. Peace God! To: Pito Da Boss aka Wiz... my n%##@, I told you I was gonna build until I make something great happen! All them late nites manifesting our thoughts, became the understanding that we've been searching for! Make that "Pito story" happen! 1 Luv my G! To: One of the Realest, most loyal dudes... that I've met in life! Timothy "KP" Wilson..... I will NEVER 4 get all the conversations, the learning process of moving correct... and staying focused, well as the staying sucka free motto! You've shown me what LOYALTY is, and in return... I gave it back without conditions! You held a n%##@ down... when I needed it most! I'm FOREVER grateful to have been blessed with your presence! They don't make ' em like us no more! I'm riding for you bruh! FREE DA GUY!!! To my: "Felony Life Street N%##@'z!" & To my: "3L Hustlaz!" Peace to my beloved... NGE (Nation of Gods and Earths). Peace to the Gods locked in the Victory Allah (Va.) penal system! "Intelligent Choice 360." Free my bro!" "Lord Jamal." Free my bro!" "Pure Black." Free my bro! "Wise One." Free my bro! "Magnetic." Free my bro! And P.E.A.C.E. to all the God's that I've traveled and build with, amongst my time in the Victory Allah (Va.) penal system. To: my entire family; the... "Bell's, Benthall's, & Taylor's." We Mobb Deep 4 Real. I love you all. It's way too many of us, to name individually! But know that the Love is genuine, and the Loyalty is 'til the death! Last but not least shout out to: S and A Publishing for giving me the opportunity to bless not only the streetz with my craft! This is only the beginning... let's go!!!

In Loving Memory of my Old Earth (Mother). Mrs. Virginia " Penny" Bell.

In Loving Memory... of someone who was more, than words could ever express!
Jarvisha D. Hardy

Dedicated to those that said I wouldn't and for all those that said I couldn't!
#LOOK AT ME NOW...

Special Dedication To: Earlean "Cookie" Morgan. Thanks for being my strength when I needed it most! I love you always Ma! We always gone be family! "FACTZ!"

As the Temptations roared through the Kenwood surround sound system, Kiem sat back on his plush Navy Blue suede Fendi sofa, guzzling shots of Asombroso The Collection singing along. "it was just my imagination, running away from me". Stuck in a daze one would think it was the tequila taking its course, after all. this wasn't no ordinary tequila retailed priced at $1,800 a bottle, just like Kiem wasn't no ordinary dude. Everything he did was with passion and purpose. Even his style was insane which earned him the nickname "Crazy Eddie". Shit after all, being from the streetz of the second biggest city in North East New Jersey, reputation was everything and it was only two rules that you live and die by. Loyalty and never snitch! No matter the situation. stay true and never rat on your guys, or anyone else regardless of the consequences. Now, 15 shots in and slumped deep on the Fendi, Kiem kicked off his all white suede Vasquez Gore - Tex boots, pulled off his all white YSL ribbed cut fitted sweater, then pulled his chrome 1911Remington 45. from his waistline cocked the hammer and then kissed the barrel.

It's 5:43 am and Bliss been hitting her nigga phone like crazy all night. It was very out of the ordinary of him not to answer, regardless of what was present at the time, he was always on deck for his greater equal half. "facts".
Worried that something wasn't right, Bliss felt an urge to rotate to her nigga spot, which was in the downtown section of Jersey City at Dixon Mills. Without haste she quickly threw on her Burberry Trench Coat, grabbed her Von Dutch clutch, the keys to her Alexander Grape Purple 550 SL coupe and stormed out her front door.
As she hopped in the Benz, she quickly reached in the console, which concealed the all black Glock compact 45. Sheba, as she referred to her Glock, stayed ready with one in the head. It was a gift to her for all her hard work and dedication, loyalty, respect, and love! Pulling off from her Grafton Ave apartment, she breezed through the streetz of the Bricks on her to Chilltown bumping the new Jadakiss feat.Rick Ross. Less than 10 minutes later she was passing Kearny Jail approaching the bridge to Rt.440, still hitting her man jack. No response. "FUCK!!!" she yelled and hit the gas running the red light. She hit a quick left as no oncoming traffic came her way, racing all the way down to Duncan Ave, where she made a quick right passing what was now the new "Duncan Projects". Thoughts instantly raced through her mind, where she remembered the seven buildings,12 story floors "A. Harry Moore" housing projects which her man called home, and many knew as Duncan Projects. To see the projects knocked down and converted anew was one thing, but the history of Duncan was another. Bliss reached Westside Ave., turned left and then made a right on Montgomery St. and took that street all the way 'til she reared off to her destination. Pulling up on the gated condos, she entered her pass code to gain access to the parking lot. Once through the gates. she quickly pulled right beside her man's oxblood colored CT6 and threw the Benz in park. With Sheba clutched tightly in the palm of her hand, her eyes quickly surveyed the parking lot before exiting the car. Everything appeared to be of normal, but her third eye sensed something else. Bliss was gutter. She was more gutter than most niggaz in the streetz, but she was a

woman all the way with it, and for that reason alone is why she was highly respected. Hopping out the Benz she paced towards the condos entrance and quickly key carded the door. Once inside the lobby, she did the knowledge to the surveillance cameras and noticed that they were pointed out of position from the front entrance, the elevators, and the lobby walkway which led to the main stairway. With her always being on point with her homework, she decided to take staircase up to the top floor where she would seek out her man's destination. As she climbed each staircase with Sheba aimed precisely ready to pop something, anxiety started to kick in as she reached the top floor. Bliss reached for the door handle and turned the knob as she opened the door and made her way into the hallway of the top floor. Pacing down the long. Carolina Blue colored carpet floor hallway, she wasted no time reaching door 211 only to discover that she did not need her key to gain entry. The lock on the door looked as if someone pried it open, and she couldn't bear the thought of what she might discover on the other side of the door. Without hesitation, she pushed her way through the door and realized that the condo was not in any disarray. Confused now because the reality didn't match her imagination, she continued to make way pass the kitchen, the bar, and into the spacious living room only to find her King knocked out on the sofa, with that pretty chrome bitch gripped in his right hand, resting on his chest. Besides a pair of Gore - Tex boots and sweater, that was thrown on the floor, well as a half bottle of Asombroso The Collection, nothing else seemed to be out of place.

As Bliss ran over to her man calling out his name. "Kiem. Kiem. bae get up!" Her eyes still searched for any potential danger. "Shit!!!" Kiem said out loud, as he awoke to his woman whose embrace was tight as ever around his neck. Reaching down to palm a nice hand full of Bliss' juicy, thick, soft ass. She let out a soft moan in his ear before saying, "bae I was worried to death. I've been blowing your phone up all night and texting to the point that I now have to get another French Manicure because my tips are done. And when I didn't get no response, you know a bitch was 'bout to dumb out. So I flew over here A.S.A.P. no rocky! But fuck all that, what happened to the lock on the door?" Bliss asked sternly. "Right now, my head is spinning like a mutha fucka. I need to rest this liquor off, and once I do we will definitely build on things, before I handle shit. Real Language!" Kiem stated. Bliss didn't question her mans' request, she was the type of woman that always listened no matter what. And that's what Kiem respected most about her. Not to mention the curves her body possessed which made every bitch envy. Coca - cola in a glass bottle because her physique resembled just that. No doubt. Bliss was one of the baddest chicks that ever float the East Coast. Both sitting in silence, Bliss rose to her feet and took Kiem by the hand as she stated, "come on bae. Let's get some rest". Kiem stood to his feet and managed to stumble down the hallway to the bedroom all without falling on top of his girl, who was doing her best to prevent him from falling face first, anywhere other than the bed. As she had a moment to herself, she smiled "Great Job. If I do say so myself" she thought.

Time was ticking but Don Smoke was making perfect time as he beat the interstate up approaching the Jersey Turnpike. Careful of his speed knowing that state troopers wait

in the cut, his eyes focused on all mirrors as he changed gears in the Gold Audi R8. Son had a need for speed and would not push nothing less than a V-10 when it came to a coupe. His handle on the wheel was like no other and he knew that no one could fuck with him when it came to popping the clutch. This is why Kiem assigned him to handle all distance travel drop offs and cash pick-ups. Timing was very important when it came to supplying the streetz. With this kind of business, as with most things, it follows a chain of command. So that anytime the chain breaks that weak link would only be as good as it's strength. Don Smoke knew and understood that very well, which is why his heart stained everything purple. Just like Kiem, he was loyal to the core. No matter the cold currents life presented he stayed true. Reaching for the backwood stuffed with 2 grams of that good Cali smoke, laying in the ash tray Don instantly fired up. With one hand on the steering wheel and straight gas in the other, thick smoke released from his nostrils as he exhaled the Lemon Berry Kush. Reminiscing, he remembered when everybody started calling him "Don Smoke", after his newfound right-hand man Kiem, added the acronym to his name, which means "Stay Motivated Obtain knowledge Everyday". It was Dons determination to be the best he possibly can, at whatever it was he did. Whether it was playing ball, hustling, working out, gambling, or just fucking hoe'z. It was also Kiem's observation of Don, which reminded him so much of himself, a fucking walking time bomb, yet humble and patient. It was also Kiem that pulled up on Don one afternoon outside on the rec yard, while doing a bid down in Yardsville. After the greeting, names were exchanged, and the rest is history! Don Smoke smiled as he recounted the bond that he created with Kiem, no doubt, that was his brother from another mother, not even death could sever. Enjoying the ride, while the marijuana blew in the breeze through the panoramic roof on the R8, Dons phone started vibrating. Without looking at his caller ID, the iPhone automated voice system stated, "Shark is calling". Hesitant to answer, the automated voice sounded again, "Shark is calling". Don gritted his teeth at the sound of Shark's name, he didn't like dude nor did he trust him, but out of respect for Kiem, he did business with the nigga only. Shark was a loudmouth, flamboyant, fake thug type of ass nigga. The type that would beat on a bitch but won't stand up to a nigga. The type that would line a nigga up if the ticket was right, and also if he knew that he could get away with it, without any repercussions. Spinning through Lincoln Park, Don took a trip down memory lane as he drove past Kiem's hood. Duncan Projects had a new structure now. The old high-rise buildings were now gone, but the concrete jungle will always have its roots. Don remembered all the late nights hustling with Kiem and shooting dice in the building's lobby. All the love he got from niggaz, well as the ladies, and all the niggaz that had died who he also had grown close to. The beefs with different project's, and nights getting chased by the Narcs, was chapter's early on in year's before he met Kiem while doing a bid for possession with intent to distribute crack cocaine.
Don Smoke was from the downtown section of the city, but had ties with damn near everyone throughout Jersey City, well as Brick City (Newark), East Orange, and a few other surrounding cities. Life was good. and knowing that his team formed like Voltron whenever need be, made life even better. Everybody operated from a distance, which gave birth to the meaning. work smarter, not harder.

hustling in the streetz together, so did their bond with each other. They used to often make sure one another was alright before saying goodnight. Gi-Gi knew Kiem had a good reputation when it came to getting money, rocking designer, or having one too many hoes. He was also a nigga not to be fucked with and played no games when it came to fucking a nigga up! In her eyes he will always remain her bro!

And she will always remain loyal, because before the hustle when she had nothing or no one she could always count on Kiem. He made sure she was good, not just with her pockets, but mentally and emotionally as well. After passing the Greensville section of Jersey City, Nice was only within minutes of the Bayonne and Jersey City border. Pulling out his phone, he called Gi-Gi. "What's hood nigga?" A soft voice asked excitedly. "Bout to pull up. Everything ready?" Nice asked. "You already know" Gi-Gi replied. "Kool cuz I gotta hit the barbershop afterwards."

"Oooh! Who you getting fresh for?" Gi-Gi asked. "Nobody particular, but I can't be all up in the club making it thunderstorm, and my shit ain't tight." Nice responded.

"Making it Thunderstorm" Gi-Gi, repeated.

"Yea! You know we throw all Jacksons on Thursday nights. Gotta show the ladies we appreciate their hard work!" Nice stated.

"We invented "T.S.T." (Thunder Storm Thursday's)" said Nice. "Y'all niggaz terrible. That's why these bitches be out here going "Kelly Bundy", whenever y'all up in the club!" Gi-Gi stated. Nice just laughed before saying "I'm out front, open the door."

Driving up Academy St., Bliss turned right on Bergen Ave. and proceeded to drive until she spotted a parking spot right outside in front of the canton. Pulling up in the empty space, Kiem jumped out before she even parked and started putting change into the parking meter. Soon as Bliss parked, Kiem walked around to the driver's side of the car opened the door and took Bliss by the hand, as she stepped out of the coupe looking flawless. Right across the street from where she had just parked, was a Gold Audi R8 parked in the opposite direction. She immediately noticed the car and said."bae looks like Don Smoke is out making his rounds". Kiem nodded

his head in agreement, knowing that his right hand man was awaiting him. Opening the door for his lady, they both entered Canton and decided to take the steps up into the restaurant, instead of the elevator. Arriving at the top entrance, Kiem seen Don Smoke from a distance over at

the bar. Instantly they were greeted by a waitress, who escorted the couple over to a corner table. As they were seated, Kiem signaled for Don Smoke to join them at the table. Bliss was surprised to see Don there, as he approached their table and gave Kiem dap. He then said what up sis. as he gave her a hug, then took a seat. They had a view of the entire restaurant and all the entrances from where they were seated. The waitress returned with three menus and took orders for any refreshments while they decided what they wanted to eat. Don Smoke ordered a vodka with lime and Kiem ordered the same, while Bliss ordered a water. Soon as the waitress left to get their drinks, Kiem got right to the point. "Bliss I know you seen how the lock was all fucked up on the door, and Don this is why I told you to meet me here. Somebody hit my crib. They took $750k in cash and 100 brickz. Whoever the fuck it was they had to be watching me or some shit because nobody knew where my condo was besides Bliss, not even you Don Smoke and you're my right-hand man." The waitress interrupted the conversation with their refreshments, as everyone then requested another round. Only this time, Bliss ordered a double Hennessey on the rocks! Don Smoke angrily asked, "Who the fuck you think it can possibly be?" "Don't know!" Kiem stated. "It could be anybody. The funny thing is nobody knew that condo was a stash house, nobody!" Kiem stated with his tone of voice turning ice cold. Bliss then stated.

"I know you don't think that I had something to do with this shit, just because I knew your location!" Storeing coldly into her eyes Kiem replied "bitch!! If I even thought that you had something to do with my fucking money or my product coming up missing. You think that ya pretty ass would still be breathing". Hurt by his harsh words and cold tone of voice, Bliss eyes started to tear up while they both locked eyes with other. After the second round of drinks, everyone ordered something to eat while they still tried to make sense of what happened. Kiem barely touched the steak lo mien, his appetite was gone knowing that he just took the biggest lost ever. Even though he still had 2.5 million in cash put away, he was now broke because he had to pay the connect for the 100 brickz. Just the thought of everything made his stomach turn upside down. Don Smoke crushed the steak and king snow crab leg's without remorse. While Bliss, still stuck in her feelings, picked through the honey lemon shrimp w/ broccoli and wild rice. Breaking the moment of silence Bliss said, "bae the night I blew ya phone up and got no response. I was worried to death cuz that'z not like you, not to respond to my calls or texts. So I instantly shot to your location to see if you was there. Soon as I entered the parking lot and seen your Cadillac parked, I pulled up right beside it and scanned the parking lot for anything out of the ordinary like you showed me. Once I witnessed everything was good, I made my way to your building entrance and entered the lobby. The first thing I noticed was the cameras pointed out of direction that they normally would be and for that reason is why I took the stairs up to your floor instead of the elevator. Soon as I reached your floor, I paced to your door and that's when I noticed the lock on the door bust open. I had my Glock ready cuz I didn't know what to expect on the other side of the door. Luckily other than your boots and sweater being out of place on the floor, you was knocked out on the sofa with your gun in your hand resting on your chest."

Kiem instantly responded. 'I remember ma! I remember now. I got to the condo and noticed the lock on the door too once I got upstairs. I never paid no mind to cameras in the lobby, but I'm definitely going to get a copy of the surveillance disc. But when I entered my spot, everything looked normal so I thought that it might have been a failed B&E. That's why I didn't notify building security, plus because of all the drugs that I thought was still there. So when I went to check the stash inside my walk in closet floor safe. Only then did I notice everything was gone. The job looks real professional because the safe was completely drilled opened. But I'm still puzzled by the fact of who the fuck knew that my stash was at that location? That exact location at that!" Kiem angrily stated. 'I bought that condo exactly 2 years ago, and I had the floor safe installed 60 days after I purchased the place. It was a custom order from K.L.S. (Keys Locks and Safes) out in

Secaucus, Nj. It's a small family own business that has operated for more than over 100yrs. But I can't put my finger on it and say that the company was behind any malice. Don Smoke interrupted. "My nigga! Somebody had to been watching you. Shit don't even sound right! You move to discrete to get caught slipping like this. But we got to get on top of this A.S.A.P." "I know man." Kiem replied. "Listen, nobody is to know about this. NOBODY!!" Kiem stated. "Mutha Fuckas are gonna die!" From the cold tone of Kiem's voice and nothing but the look of death deep within his eyes, Bliss and Don Smoke both knew that Kiem meant every word. Even if it claimed his own life. "Bliss, I need you to make a few moves for me!" Kiem stated. Reaching into his pocket, he pulled out a set of keys and before handing them to her, he said. "pack all ya personal shit, I'll call you with the address". He then placed the keys into the palm of her hands. "New House?" Bliss excitedly asked out loud. "Yea". Kiem answered. "Can't have you laying by yourself no more, it's too dangerous and too easy for a nigga to target me through you. You understand?" Kiem asked. Bliss nodded her head in agreement, not only because she understood her man's point of view, but because she also understood the savage that he was very well capable of becoming. The trio then exited the restaurant, only this time using the elevator on their way downstairs. Once outside, Kiem told Bliss that he would get with her shortly. He then kissed her softly on the lips, then escorted her to the driver's side of her car, assuring she pulled off safely. Seeing the Benz fade in distance, Kiem and Don hopped in the R8. Conversation over a backwood stuffed with Moon Rock, ,their minds started to detect one another as they put the pieces of the puzzle together. They both laughed at the situation, knowing that it was 'bout to be a slaughter. "My nigga. I got to switch shit up!" Kiem stated. "Because that would make a nigga expose himself and wanna turn it up a notch too. And once that happens, I'll have my target." Kiem expressed. "Factz." Don Smoke said. "Big Factz." Kiem replied. "The average nigga is tender dick. Straight bitch made. You can do just 'bout whatever to a nigga and still walk the streetz. But if you fuck their bitch, they're gonna want to go to war. And niggaz pillow talk so it's only a matter of time!" Kiem stated. "And who ever hit my crib think that's the end of my reign, but if they only knew, that was just the end of something small that just now birthed something big."

Working two pots on the electric glass top stove, Nice was whipping one pie into two. Within a matter of minutes, he turned 500 grams of cocaine into 1000 grams of crack. The cocaine was so pure that he could easily stepped on it three times. tripling the weight. Shit with product coming straight out of Bolivia 90% raw, hands down, Kiem and his squad best work North to South. Following that same recipe, he performed magic again while Gi-Gi started to bust down the first brick and bag it up. Amazed at his wrist work in the kitchen, the only other person she seen whip like that was Kiem. Thinking to herself, that had to be a family recipe the way they whipped, 'cuz nobody whipped like they did. As fast as she bagged the product and hauled it to it's destinations it was gone. Never was it a complaint, the product spoke for itself. And her runners always handled business. After Nice dumped the second pot and sat the brick on the table in front of her his worked was done. He then gave Gi-Gi a hug and told her to be safe as she followed him towards the front door, so that she could lock it behind him. Once Nice got in the truck, he texted Blades "on my way 2u now". Less than a minute, Blades hit back "come through". Blades had been Nice barber for years and worked at "Anyway you want it". "Anyway you want it" was one of the most popular barbershops in Jersey City. It's name defined its reputation, and drew clientele from everywhere.

Back in Brick City, Bliss wasted no time gathering all her designer. So excited that Kiem wanted her at home with him every night, she couldn't help but shove whatever the Louis Vuitton suit cases and duffle bags allowed inside. Without a care; she stuffed black trash bags full with boots, heels, sandals, and sneakers until her shoe racks were completely empty. With all her designer packed up and ready for its new location, she went to her bedroom wall vent which was a secret drop box, and removed the magnetic vent cover. Reaching inside she took out five rubber band stocks of Franklin's, which was her own money that she'd been saving up for over three years now. 50k was good for any female that could hold her own, minus having a nigga that had that bag! Still reaching inside she took out ten more stocks of Franklin's, which was the money Kiem had given to her, to support her dreams of opening her very own women's academy teaching all women that experienced trauma, how to provide for themselves, get proper education, job skills, and to become independent. 100k was more than enough money to make her dream a reality, but Bliss wanted to do it on her own to show her man that she wasn't no needy bitch and just fucking with him 'cuz of the money. Her loyalty to him was 'til the death! Bliss quickly put the money inside a Black Hermes Tote, then tossed a small velvet sack inside before stuffing two pictures of her and Kiem and one of her late mother inside. Tears flooded her eyes as she remembered very little of her mother, who died in a tragic car accident when she was only three years old. Her father was deported back to Panama upon his release from federal prison, for embezzlement and credit card fraud when she was eleven years old. Left with no one and in foster care until she was forced to flee custody at age sixteen, for stabbing her case worker in the face for trying to molest her. With no food, clothing, or shelter, all alone in the streetz. Bliss remembered "Ai'Adore, who took her in and showed her how to manipulate the streetz. With no kids of her own, Ai'Adore provided food, clothes, and shelter and loved and took care of Bliss, like she was her own. Bliss grew very close to the woman who she called aunty. And regardless of her lifestyle, Bliss never judged her. Ai'Adore was on her shit. She made her money making niggaz cum. All of her clients consisted of corporate gentlemen; judges, lawyers, doctors, bondsmen, congressmen, and a few owners of various sports teams. Ai'Adore was no cheap trick. Her time was valued at five thousand dollars and better. And if a john wanted her for the whole night or two, that was an easy fifteen to twenty five thousand dollars made. Bottom line, Bliss never wanted for shit, up until she laid eyes on Kiem four years later when he came to buy a few guns from aunty. From that moment on, the streetz labeled them "201 Fly". Still thinking back, Bliss remembered times when aunty joked with Kiem about making him her boy toy. It was all for a good laugh and never disrespect. It's been nine years now since Ai'Adore and myself discovered each other, and six years out of that nine, that Kiem and I had been committed to one another. Even through all the trauma. I knew that I would make it through hell and come out right! Bliss stated to herself. With her thoughts interrupted by the ringing of her phone, she seen that it was Kiem calling as his name flashed across the caller Id. "Hey bae!" Bliss stated as she answered the phone. "Everything good?" Kiem asked. "Of course. All packed up and ready." "Great". Kiem replied. The address is "7781 Plainfield Ave." the house is up in North Bergen. I'll get with you early in the am after I make a few runs gotta see who's talking. "Be safe. I love you!" Bliss stated. "Love you back ma." Kiem replied before hanging up.

Pulling up on the corner of Ocean Ave and Grant Ave., Nice Parked right in front of the infamous barbershop. Reaching under his driver seat, he grabbed the camouflage Glock 40 and tucked it in his waistline. Hopping out the Range, he dapped a few niggaz up who stood outside in front of the barbershop while making his way through the entrance. Once inside, he dapped more niggaz up, before making his way over to his barber's chair, and showing his barber some love too. "What's shaking?" Blades asked as he shook hands with Nice. "(T.S.T.) Thunder Storem Thursday." Nice replied, while taking a seat in the chair. "Already!" Blades stated as he wrapped the barber's smock around Nice and went straight to work. Getting the usual, Nice overheard niggaz talking 'bout Club Angels and how Shark got all the V.I.P. sections bought out. Paying closer attention, he listened as one of the niggaz mentioned Nicco's name, who was also a slime ball type of nigga who ran with Shark. Not knowing Kiem's situation, and not thinking nothing out of the ordinary. Nice paid the conversation no mind. After finishing the shape up on Nice low cut cesar. Blades lined up his moustache and goatee, then brushed him off with the barber's talc. After removing the smock, Nice reached in his pocket and pulled out a blue face and put it in his hand.as he dapped Blades up and passed the money off for his skilled services. Looking in the wall mirror as he exited the barbershop, Nice knew that his shit was tight. Pulling out his phone while walking to the driver's side of his truck. He called Don Smoke as he got in behind the wheel. "Yo! Yo!" Don Smoke stated as he answered his phone." My nigga we definitely lit tonight, no doubt about it!" Nice stated as he continued. "Just left the barbershop, heard that nigga Shark got all the V.I.P. on smash at Club Angels tonight. Plus Nicco is 'posed to be the new plug now at a better price." "Word!!" Don Smoke replied. "Look I'm with bro now we gone dip and link up at the club. Everything's everything though?" Don Smoke asked. "Always" replied Nice. Pulling heavy on the backwood, Don Smoke looked at Kiem then passed the blunt before saying "That was Nice, shit crazy right now. That bitch nigga Shark got the whole V.I.P. at Angels tonight and the nigga Nicco somehow is supposed to be plugged with better prices." Choking off the smoke Kiem managed to say, "what the fuck". Then exhaled heavily before saying "how the fuck Nicco plugged? None of this shit adding up my nigga, I need to find out who and how he even got a connect!" Kiem aggressively stated. Just last week, both of them niggaz was buying from us and now Nicco name buzzing. But peep the fly shit Kiem stated. Shark just got two chickens from you two days ago and my crib got hit exactly one day before that. Now if Nicco really got that work Shark would have spent the money with him, instead of us for two reasons.1).because they both grimy as fuck and run together and 2) because they both some greedy ass niggaz, just like pigs, They'll eat anything!" Kiem stated. "And if Nicco prices are better, why not keep the money in the circle? You feel me." Kiem asked. "I feel you bro." Don Smoke answered. "Now check this fly shit! Let's say Nicco do got that work but ain't tell Shark nothing until he can come up with a blueprint, for how he got his on shit. Like you said they both greedy as fuck and knowing that Shark would be looking for a handout, and Nicco don't play fair with nobody!" Don Smoke stated. "Say no more Don." Kiem replied. "I can't point the finger them niggaz just yet, but I'm damn sure not canceling 'em out either. But I have to get this money to the connect like yesterday. I got it all, but I'm dead ass broke once I empty the safe. All we working with is the cash you got on deck, and the cash coming in from Gi-Gi runners. My nigga this shit is like starting from ground zero all over again. But my good word we 'bout to turn up to the max. This comeback is gone be greater than Jordan comeback wearing the # 45."

Turning into Dixon Mills, Don Smoke drove up to the locked gates as Kiem gave him the entry codes to enter the parking lot. Once the electric gates opened, Kiem directed Don to where his Cadillac was parked. Standing outside the Audi, their eyes scanned the entire parking lot for anything that seemed abnormal. As they reached the condominiums front entrance, Kiem key carded the door as him and Don entered the lobby. With no one present at the lobby desk. Kiem told Don Smoke to look, as he pointed to the surveillance cameras that was now positioned back in their proper place. The front entrance, the elevators, and the lobby walkway. "The fucking cameras wasn't like that when me and Bliss left. And this fat Spanish, doughnut eating, mutha fucka Ario ain't even working!" Kiem angrily stated. "What type of security they have monitoring this place anyway? Kiem questioned sarcastically. Don just shrug his shoulders and continued to do his homework, as they walked to the elevator's. Waiting for either elevator to hit the lobby floor, Don Smoke asked Kiem. "Bro! You sure nobody been following you?" 'Cuz from what you told me thus far it seems like someone's been watching you!" "My nigga! I'm sure nobody's been following me." Kiem replied. "I've been at this spot for two years, and I'm sure that nobody followed Bliss here. Because I can count on one hand, every time that she ever came here. For instance, let's say someone did follow her here, how the fuck would they know which condo she was entering when there's no guest log in. My point exactly!" Don Smoke exclaimed before dropping this jewel. "Someone's been watching you. they had to know ya line of work, ya exact location, well as the fact that you had a built in floor safe installed". "This wasn't just no regular hit this shit was personal!" Don Smoke stated. Puzzled by what Don just said. Kiem racked his brain striving to make sense of the situation being personal. Deep in thought the elevator bell sounded as the doors opened on one elevator and Ms. Estelvo stepped off storeing Kiem deep in his eyes before greeting him, and introducing herself to Don Smoke. "Hello, Mr. Pairings." she said, as she shook Kiem's hand, then extended her hand to Don Smoke and introduced herself. "Hello I am Ms.Karma Estelvo!" "Nice to meet you Ms. Estelvo.my name is Don." "A pleasure to meet you Don." Ms. Estelvo replied. "Mr. Pairings can you and your guest follow me to the lobby office, we have an issue that needs to be addressed." Focused on this bitch word play and body language. Don Smoke had no idea that she owned the property. But he quickly bore witness to how her eyes were glued to Kiem. As everyone entered the office, Ms. Estelvo then informed

another thirty ounces between two more zip lock bags before placing the last twelve ounces into a large white castle paper bag. Gi-Gi wasted no time stuffing the zip locks inside her black and silver Michael Kors tote, as she carried the white castle paper bag in hand stepping outside her residence. A couple steps within reach from the driver side door, she jumped in the emerald green Aviator and tossed the Michael Kors into the front passenger seat. Easily pulling off in the Lincoln looking pretty she took Broadway all the way down 'til she reached Lord Ave and stopped at her first destination. Pulling out her phone Gi-Gi texted, "downstairs". Then sent another text."10mins. BOF" (Be Out Front). Less than a minute had passed before "Bandz" came outside and hopped in the Lincoln. "Bitch, what's mobbin?" Bandz asked. "Mind Elevation". Gi-Gi replied before handing over one of the zip lock bagz containing five ounces. Reaching into her pantyline, Bandz pulled out a pink rubber banned knot of twenties and gave it to Gi-Gi. before stashing the zip lock bag down in her panties. Eyeing the money. Gi-Gi could easily tell that it was five thousand. Besides all her runners never came short, and they all had one thing in common, they were all women! Each of them had their own drip which gave definition to their crown, that the streetz blessed them with called. "The 7 Sexes!" "Yo! Tell me why I saw imaginary playa and he was talking dis major key shit like he was DJ Khaled or some fuckin body!" Bandz said. "Who? Nicco?" Gi-Gi asked, as she laughed because everybody knew that he was Shark's shadow, fronting like he a top notch nigga in the streetz. "Yea!!" Bandz replied. "The nigga was talking reckless 'bout how he always wanted a real bitch like me, and now he got his bag right he can afford to take care of me. Then the nigga gone come out his mouth and say I got ten bands for you right now if we fuck! So I asked the nigga, how u got ten bands fa sum pussy and u barely got ten different pair of jeans? Then he just pulled out 10k with the paper band still wrapped round the money, and gone say." Pink Bandz & Nicco", how that sound? Before I could even get the words."Dead Ball" out my mouth, the nigga tossed me the money and said clean ya self up.I'm throwing a party next Friday, at "Main Event". I expect to see you there and bring ya boss with you. Tell her I got value prices like Wal-Mart." Insulted by a clown nigga demeanor, Gi-Gi spit out her driver's side window to rid of the bad taste she had in her mouth, then said to Bandz, "Unless he won the lottery over night, I don't know whose dick he on that got him feeling like he boss'd up now. Then to make matter's worst, the nigga gone try to cash you out for the pussy like you some type of Thot-Bot. Woww!!" Gi-Gi exclaimed. I said the same shit 2 myself! Bandz stated. But we not stressing no tender dick nigga." Bandz said as she continued "Just think! If he offered 10k to fuck and really got that work he gone chase these pantiez 'til they drop. Which means his ass stand a better chance surviving a head on collision, instead of speedin behind me!" Bands stated. "Okay!!" Gi-Gi replied. But we doin Main Event said Pink Bandz. Shiittt."The 7 Sexes", we are Main Event!! Bandz stated with confidence. "I'll let the ladies know what it is." Gi-Gi said as she gave Bandz a hug, then watched her get out the truck and disappear back into the building.

Making way to the next stop, she rolled up on "Storemy" who was standing outside of 3rd St. projects, waiting for the dropping off. Contemplating on what Pink Bandz just told her, she unintentionally ignored Storemy's question until she asked again!

"Get it? You okay ma? Looks like you got some shit on your mind!" "Nah I'm good." Gi-Gi replied. "Just handling things you know! But we shaking shit up at "Main Event" next Friday. The whole squad. This sucka ass nigga Nicco throwing a party like he man of the year." "Whaattt??!! This nigga throwing parties now. This shit gotta be a hoax. The nigga never thrown nothing in his life! Not even his hands up to fight when he got knocked out!" Storemy stated. "Please don't remind me" said Gi-Gi, as she exchanged the white castle bag in one hand and received a thick stack of bills in the other. "I gotta roll Storemy. be safe out here!" Gi-Gi expressed. "You too Gi-Gi." Storemy replied back.

Taking Kennedy Blvd. in route to her next drop off, she decided to call Kiem just to see if he heard any of the gossip. Five, six, seven. dial tone! Nigga pick up.she said out loud, as she hit him back on speed dial. One, two, voicemail. "Nigga I know you ain't ignoring my calls, and I know you ain't in no pussy. the fuck!!!" Gi-Gi said angrily, as she called back she heard the voicemail say "yo. if I ain't answer my phone either I'm busy, or I don't fuck with you. And if I don't fuck with you, what you even calling me for? I don't do favors". Damn! Straight voicemail. Gi-Gi knew Kiem was taking care something important, 'cuz he always answer whenever she calls. So she couldn't but smile to herself at his cocky ass voicemail, knowing that it was nothing other than truth. Pulling up on 20th. St. and Kennedy Blvd., Gi-Gi parked and waited for "Whyte Diamondz" to step outside the bar, so she can make the drop and proceed with the last run. Within seconds, the 5 foot 6, bloande hair, green eyed, ton complected, Whyte Diamondz, stepped outside the bar and strutted over to the Aviator. Her diamond designer necklace sent shots of bling everywhere as the sun touched the curvy melee of round brilliants set exquisitely in an art deco setting. While her diamond drop earrings with Asher cut and Princess cut stones, complimented her face so beautifully. Gi-Gi knew that Diamondz was the flyest white chick that ever roamed the streetz of Bayonne. Plus she had clout that was uandeniable. With her measurements being 36-24-46 it was self-explanatory why most dudes wish they could enjoy the ride. "Get it-Get-it. what's good ma?" Whyte Diamondz asked. Gi-Gi replied. "You! You and your Diamondz, Diamond!" "Thanks!" Whyte Diamondz said as she climbed into the passenger's seat of the truck. Diggin' in her purse she took out a legal sized envelope containing 30k, with a strip of black electrical tope wrapped around it, and gave it to Gi-Gi. In return. Gi-Gi handed her two of the zip lock bagz totaling 30 ounces, and watched as she carefully secured both zip locks into her purse. Oh yea! We hittin' "Main Event" next Friday it's a party going on, said Gi-Gi. "Oooh.Nice keeping secrets now? Why he ain't promote this early on?" Diamondz asked. "Your guess is as good as mine" said Gi-Gi. "But Nicco is the one throwing the party, and he got the nerve to send me a direct invite". "Sounds like Nicco tryna move in on someone." Diamondz giggled! "Yea and it damn sure ain't me." Gi-Gi replied. "Well let me slide so I can get rollin'!" Diamondz stated as she got out the truck. "I'll been I touch Gi-Gi." Looking in her rearview mirror, Gi-Gi could easily she behind her in distance from where she was parked. Making sure no traffic came her way, she pulled off then turned right on 21st St and drove ahead until she reached Broadway, then made a left and proceeded 'til she reached E. 50th St. Sitting at the marble table across from Oscar Vyntura, Kiem sat motionless as the two titanium briefcases rested on the table directly in front of his connect. Waiting upon Roberto's return, Oscar opened the brief cases one after the next, revealing 2.5 millon dollars in cash. Pleased by Kiem's success, Oscar waived for his men to clap their hands out of respect for Kiem, as he did the same. Returning with a silver serving tray in his hand, Roberto served Kiem a double shot of Casa Noble Reposado, as he did Oscar. Then poured the men whom stood surrounded around the table a drink. "A toast to my most loyal and trustworthy friend." Oscar commanded! As everyone raised their drink. "to loyalty, royalty, power, and respect" Oscar stated, as everyone tossed their drinks back. With the soothing smooth taste of vanilla and lemon grass, the drink was very much liked and appreciated by everyone, from another round of applause. Looking Oscar dead into his eyes, Kiem stated. "I need a moment of privacy with you". Signaling for his men to leave the room, Oscar poured Kiem and then himself another round as his men left them alone. Once the door closed, "What seems to burden you my friend?" Oscar asked. "Listen, my condo was broken into and my safe completely emptied, 750k and 100 kilos. The same 100 kilos I received from you. I haven't got a direct lead as of yet, but the streetz is watching and it's only a matter of time before they start talking. But what puzzles me the most is the fact that no one, I mean no one, knew that my condo was a stash house. The safe was completely drilled open, looks like it was done by a professional or some shit. And that cash I just paid you, it wasn't profit from the 100 kilos, that was all the money I had saved up on my own. So once I realized the shipment was gone, it was nothing I could do but give you everything I had to make good on my word!" Kiem expressed seriously. "My friend I appreciate your sincere honestly! Your loyalty is measured greatly by your actions." Oscar stated. "Tell me how can I be of any service to you? Two hundred, three hundred kilos perhaps? perhaps one million dollars in cash and five hundred kilos? Can you handle five hundred kilos?" Oscar asked. "I can handle whatever. It's not the weight that I'm concerned with. Five hundred kilos, I'll bench press that shit!" Kiem stated as he stored at Oscar and continued talking. "My issue is whoever got my fucking money and that product is dead! It's already written in stone and their blood I will require at thy hands." Storeing Kiem attentively in his eyes, Oscar knew that his word was bond, regardless to whom or what, and that he was more than prepared for any bloodshed that would occur. "Very well addressed my friend!" Oscar stated. "Take the million in cash and reevaluate your situation. Look at it as a gift and always remember. loyalty is everything! The shipment Will be awaiting you, the same pick up location, 500 kilos. Roberto!" Oscar called out to one of his most humble servants. Appearing within seconds, Oscar made a fist with his left hand as Roberto took notice, then quickly disappeared. Focusing on what just happened, Kiem knew that it was some type of language being spoken, but only in codes. Sort of like that secret society type of shit, he thought to himself. Within five minutes, Roberto reappeared, only this time with a Virgil Abloh's 2054 Louis Vuitton, 3D-monogram bag. Placing the bag on the table, Roberto instantly vanished. like he was never there. Opening the bag to reveal it's contents, Oscar smiled as he pushed the bag across the table to Kiem. "One million cash, it's yours. Business is good, loyalty is better!" Oscar stated, as he shook hands with Kiem. Grabbing the bag up off the table, Kiem saluted Oscar before exiting the door at his 17-acre estate. All type of shit raced through Kiem's mind, as he walked down the marbled steps towards the yellow brick driveway, and up to the driver's side of his car door. Soon as he opened the door, he placed the Louis Vuitton, 3-D monogram bag on the passenger's side floor then positioned himself behind the wheel as he pushed start the CT-6. Heading down the long curvy driveway, Kiem pulled out his phone and seen that Gi-Gi been calling back to back. Hitting her back on speed dial. instantly she answered. "Heyyy boo!" she said. "You funny!" Kiem stated. "What up tho?" I see that you been calling, but I was handling something important otherwise you know I would have answered at God speed. "I know." Gi-Gi replied. "But catch this wave! I just got word that Nicco is throwing a party at Main Event next Friday. Did you know anything 'bout it?" "Fuck No!!!" Kiem replied. "But let that lollypop do him, I know Nice toxed his sucka ass. That's another thing! Why Nice ain't say nothing 'bout promoting this bitch nigga party?" Gi-Gi asked. "I don't have a clue." Kiem answered. "Then on top of that the nigga not only sent Bandz an invite, he told her to bring her boss and let me know, he's moving for the low." Gi-Gi said. Veins started jumping out Kiem's forehead as he grew angered behind what Gi-Gi just told him. "Look slide through Club Angels tonight, I need to holla!" Kiem stated. "Already!" Gi-Gi replied, before hanging up. Now thinking about the phone call Nice made to Don, about over hearing niggaz talk about Shark having the whole V.I.P. tonight at Club Angels, and how Nicco is plugged with better prices. Then his conversation with Don Smoke, and the statement Don made."750k plus 100 brickz, somebody's all the way up". Slowly everything started to make sense. Greed is what destroys most men. Kiem thought to himself. Knowing a greedy mutha fucka dies a miserable death! Kiem seen it happen several times in several different states. Greedy ass niggaz getting their tops knocked the fuck off!

Before calling Nice on speed dial, Kiem knew that his older brother had no knowledge of Nicco's party, otherwise he would have mentioned it, so he knew it was wise not to question his brother's promotion on the party, but took another route to make him aware of the party being held at his club. Touching his name on the speed dial display. "What's good Kiem?" Nice asked as he answered. "On my way to check on Bliss." Kiem replied. "Just caught a wave that Nicco's throwing a party at ya club next Friday." "Yea right!" Nice stated. "Nah big bro. I'm dead ass serious." Kiem said. "It fucked me up when I first heard about it, 'cuz I'm like Nice ain't stay nothing 'bout this one. Then I thought about the convo you overheard at the barbershop, and if it's any truth to it about the sucka ass nigga being plugged. He's gonna try to rock niggaz to sleep unexpectedly by throwing a party at the city's hottest club. Just think!!!" Kiem vividly expressed. "Everybody be at "Main Event" on Friday's, everybody! Every nigga that's touching any kind of paper, all the bitches, then your got the old headz that be chasing that young pussy, spending money all night! So it's a win-win situation for the nigga to expose himself begin plugged for the low." Kiem stated. "Lil bro! If that nigga is the plug now, who the fuckin is the socket?" Nice asked. "That nigga had to backdoor some shit, 'cuz who in their right mind would fuck with a supa slimey nigga!" Nice stated. "That much we don't know." said Kiem. "But what I do know is I'm 'bout to switch speedz. Can't be in the same lane with a lame brain nigga!" Kiem stated. "The whole squad is 'bout to get richer and I ain't getting stepped on, I'll murder 'bout minez!" Kiem stated coldly. Nice saw the look on his brothers face over the other end of the phone and knew that Kiem was not a regular person when pushed. "Bro! I'm gonna check the clubs e-mails and see if this nigga is reserved for next Friday. I'll let you know something soon as I find out anything. Usually Tokyo handles all the bookings and reservations, but she hasn't informed me 'bout promoting no up and coming party, unless dude didn't want the promotion. But I'm definitely gone get back to you on this!" Nice stated. "I'll catch you at Angels then. Crew love!" Kiem replied, before their lines went dead.

With all her belongings crammed up in the trunk and scattered across the back seat and floor of her car, Bliss was happily on her way to the address that Kiem had given her. Anxious to see what her new residence looked like she pulled out her phone and Googled the address using Google Earth, to get a sneak preview. Surprised that nothing showed up for the address, she googled it again. Now thinking that the address was wrong or something, she instantly grew antsy and stepped on the accelerator. Talking to herself under her breath. Bliss cussed Kiem out, while thinking the craziest shit. "Why the fuck this nigga give me an address that don't even register?" "What type of shit he dealing with?" "This nigga wanna play games now!" "He on some real kid shit like I won't spin on his fucking ass!" "I'm not one of these head over heels, dick chasing bitches out here. Nah! I'm lying you do fuck me good but what the fuck Kiem!" Fighting herself mentally, Bliss barely noticed that she had reached Plainfield Ave already. "Dammnnn!! I must have been flying." she said out loud while making the turn on Plainfield Ave. Looking for the address, she continued to drive growing weary of every house number going up, and still not seeing the address given. Still driving. she suddenly witnessed the number 7781 in bold script on the front door of a rust colored brick, double car garage house. Quickly turning into the driveway, Bliss put the car in park as her fingers fumbled through her bag to retrieve the door keys. Excitedly rushing through the threshold, Bliss was stunned by the beautiful crystal chandelier that hung from the ceiling foyer. Making her presence known, she hurried down the hallway reaching the living room, only to discover how beautifully decorated it was. The dark brown and beige Italian leather and suede sofa was accommodated by it's love seat and matching Ottoman. The glass coffee tables were skillfully crafted with gold trim, the same trim as the 14-foot beige silk curtains, which draped down to the carpeted floor. Right above the fireplace sat an 80inch Sony TV mounted to the wall, with theater surround sound that was Bluetooth capable. Deep in thought, Bliss knew Kiem had good taste when it came to cars, fashion, and jewelry! But the way this living room was furnished was different. Even though his condo was plush, one would think of it to be a bachelor's pad aka "Hoe House". But just standing in this living room alone let her know that Kiem was ready to have a home. Breaking her train of thought. she searched the rest of the house looking for the bedroom and discovered four! After curiously looking into each room, she instantly fell into love with the master bedroom. It was huge. A king size bed laced with Versace linen, and a matching Versace rug on the floor. A huge Versace mirror hung on the wall, which was also trimmed in gold. The marble countertop dresser and nightstands were designed with perfection. The walk-in-closet was spacious with designer hanging everywhere, that still had their price tags attached. Bliss checked out some of the labels which ranged from Saint Laurent, Dior Men, Bottega Veneto, Ferragamo, Givenchy, Gucci, and Louis Vuitton just to name a few! She could do nothing but smile knowing that Kiem stayed on his fly shit. Very impressed, she tried to envision how he'd look in the all black linen Givenchy two piece suit. She had never seen him in casual before, so it was hard for her to paint a picture mentally.

Surfing through the channels on the 75inch Sony XBR LED panel TV., Don Smoke couldn't find anything worth watching. With only a few hours of down time left, he decided to twist a backwood. Counting the money as he neatly stocked it in the safe. 300k from the eight down in Delaware, 75k for the two I sold Shark. Three hundred and seventy-five thousand. "ALL THERE!!!" He said out loud to himself. Pulling on the backwood, his mind went to work as he watched how slow the backwood burned every time he pulled on it. Reminiscing about everything that he heard and witnessed with his down eyes, Don Smoke was no fool when it came to picking a person. He could tell Ms. Estelvo was a real live piece of shit and had it something bad when it came to his brother from another. Determined to put his finger on whatever the problem was, he knew better that this wasn't just no regular kick a nigga door in type of shit. This was personal and the best was yet to come. Reaching up into his closet, he pulled out a black and gold Glock .40 then put a thirty stick in it. Making sure it was ready with one in the head, he pulled out another extendo and made sure it had a full thirty clip. Grabbing the red suede Prada jacket, and the pair of Navy Blue Balmain jeans off their hangers, he then reached for the red Prada shirt and ripped the price togs off everything, as he laid the clothes across the end of his bed before lacing up the red patent leather Prada sneakers. With nothing left to do besides catch a few hours of rest. Don Smoke laid back across the end of his bed and dozed off!

Parking in front of the building on E. 50th St., Gi-Gi stepped out the Aviator, walked towards the building entrance, and vanished into the building's lobby. Making her way up the first flight of steps, she reached the second floor and knocked on the door. Looking through the peep hole, "Passion Shooter" seen that it was "Get it-Get it" and opened the door without asking who it was! They exchanged hugs as Gi-Gi got slapped with the strong aroma of straight gas being blown. Reaching the front room, she was greeted by "Rose XL", and "N.D.A."(pronounced Iandi'A). "Damn bitches! Y'all burning this bitch down! "Somebody call the fire department please!" N.D.A. said sarcastically in response to Gi-Gi. "And look at you XL, you know damn well ya ass is to phat for them lil ass coochie cutters you got on!" Gi-Gi stated. "Hey! Hey! Hey!" As she twerked, making her ass clap like a live studio audience. Rose XL was built ford tough and from as women's point of view, Gi-Gi knew that and gave her her props! After all standing at 5'7,with measurements of 34-28-50 it's no wonder why the streetz gave XL after her name. Enjoying the smoke as the blunt rotated, Gi-Gi removed the last five zips from her MK purse and placed 'em on the table. While Passion Shooter counted out twenty five thousand, N.D.A. grabbed two boxes of rubber bands, a box of gems, and two cases of Gp45's (crack valves), so her and Rose XL could start bagging up! Passion joined in to help once the count was right, and Gi-Gi had the money. The gem stores chopped chunks

250k and all I had to do was empty some rich niggaz safe. The shit was too easy! But why would this bitch want Bliss dead? He questioned himself. He couldn't figure it out, no matter how hard he thought about it. But what he did know for sure is that he didn't want no kind of problems with Kiem. None whatsoever!! So killing Bliss was dead! Straight out the question! Not giving a fuck either, 'cuz he had the cash upfront already. And now that he had more cocaine than in his dreams, he didn't care 'bout handling his obligations. But if he only knew that the bitch he'd been doing sneak business with was more ruthless than he could ever imagine. This was the life that he dreamed of. money, cars, bitches, respect, and everything else. Smiling to himself, he continued to think. Only this time. he thought out loud to himself, while constantly checking himself out in his rearview. "It's on bitches. I'm 'bout to run these streetz. I got 100 brickz and I got my money up! Everybody know how the slimy grimy gets down. The city gone be on my dick come next Friday. I'm supplying the streetz. Me Nicco the don!" As he laughed at his thoughts being cockier than Debo!

Backing into the old engine repair and tire shop, Kiem wasted no time closing the garage door with the touch of the remote, as it automatically locked. Grabbing the 3-D monogram bag,he then grabbed the duffel out the truck, and made his way through the shop. Reaching the back office, he entered through the door, then entered through another door. which presented the tiny studio. Smiling as he remembered how he use to frequent occupy the small space. He tossed both bags onto the twin size bed, before reaching underneath and grabbing the Glock.43. Releasing its clip he reached back under the bed and grabbed the two extensions, and examined them both. Making sure they each had 30 rounds, combined for the full 60 shots! Walking back through both doors and back out into the shop, he opened his trunk, then opened the back doors to one of the repair shop customized vans. As he lifted the back floor panel of the van, Kiem felt a rush like he never felt in his life, knowing that he was back on top. Looking at the 500 kilos neatly stocked, he knew that from this moment on his life would never be the same. He knew that his loyalty had taken him to a level that only made men can operate on. Grabbing a couple of old laundry sacks from off the floor, he started filling 'em up with the work. With six and a half laundry sacks full of cocaine, he laid three of the sacks across the back of his trunk. then put another three on top of that. After closing the trunk. he placed the last laundry sack on his driver's side back floor, before making his way back through the shop again. He entered through the first door, then through the next, until he was standing back in the middle of his tiny domain. Taking his fit out of the Gucci duffle, he stripped down and took a quick shower. The stand in shower was tighter than a crawl space and reminded him of an old fashion telephone booth. He had no choice but to laugh every time his elbows hit the walls, because he knew that it was a tight situation, but it did its job.

Fresh out the shower Kiem threw on some Bleu De` Chanel, then started getting ready as he reached for his phone. Waking up to the ringing of his phone "what up?" Don Smoke asked, as Kiem's voice sounded through the speaker. "You ready to rotate my G?" Kiem asked. "Give me thirty. I just got up! Bout to hit this shower and get dripped. I'll meet you in the parking lot where we normally park at." said Don Smoke. "Already!"

Kiem replied as their lines went dead. Snatching up the clothes he had on prior to changing, Kiem stuffed everything inside the Gucci duffle bag and zipped it closed. Now calling Bliss on speed dial, "Hey baby!" She answered excitedly, and continued on, "This house is beautiful, I love it! The bedroom is gorgeous. I love the whole Versace scene. Everything is spacious. But why four bedrooms bae?" "So I can sleep in one of the other rooms, whenever I get tired of your ass!" Kiem sarcastically replied as he laughed! Not feeling his sarcastic ass remark, she decided to shoot one back at him. "Ooh! How you gone get tired of this deep throat, and this supa soaker? What you gay now??" Bliss asked as she laughed her ass off!! "Whaattt???" Kiem harshly asked! "Aight then nigga! Don't come for me, 'cuz you know I fires back!" Bliss arrogantly stated. "Ma look! Forget all this dumb shit. we'll finish this in the bedroom. I likes that!! You know I handles mine. But check! I need to switch. meet me across the street from the court house, in the back of the parking lot now! I'm on my way bae! Bliss replied. Tucking the Glock.43 in his back waistline, Kiem then put on his jacket to conceal the weapon and it's stick. before reaching to pick the second one up off the bed. Putting the second stick in his inside jacket pocket, he grabbed both duffle bags up and headed towards his car. Placing both bags on the passenger's side floor, Kiem knew that he had to move quick and precise because twelve be out looking for anything that looks suspicious during the late hours in that part of the city he was traveling from. Starting the Cadillac, he opened the garage door and exited. Riding down Palisades Ave., Kiem's phone started ringing. He knew it was Gi-Gi calling as her name flashed across the car touch screen."what's good ma?" Kiem asked.as he answered the call. "Checking on you!" Gi-Gi replied. "I'm in rotation now. I'll be at the club in 'bout 15 mins." Gi-Gi stated. "Yea! I'm not that far behind you myself!" Kiem said in return. "Nice should already be up in the spot. He got this TOB (Thot Ass Bitch), that's the main attraction there, so you know how that go. But I'm 'bout to skate through this tunnel, so.I'll get with you shortly. Don Smoke should be arriving any minute now too! You'll see his car parked to your left of the club's entrance, once you enter the parking lot." Kiem stated. "Okay boo! I'll be waiting for you." Gi-Gi said as she laughed. "Ma look let's not fuck up our friendship, or our business partnership. Besides, this ain't what you want!" Kiem stated. "It is, trust me, it is!" Gi-Gi replied. "Ya ass crazy girl! I'll be there in a few. One!"

Pulling into the parking lot, Kiem spotted Bliss parked way in the back, just a few spaces from the pay booth. The lot was barely vacant, and it was way past business hours, so the booth attendant had long been gone. This was the perfect blind spot for any type of illegal activity to take place, 'cuz the surrounding streetz were dark and so was the parking lot except for one sign that read "Park Here" at the entrance of the lot. Kiem pulled right up besides Bliss and turned off his lights, but left the car running as he got out and walked over to the passenger's side of the Benz and got in. "Hey ma!" He said as he gave her a quick peck on the lips and kept the convo short. "Listen, guard that Louis Vuitton bag with your life! Park the car inside the garage and activate the alarm system on the house soon as you get inside. I'll handle the baggage when I get home." "I got you Daddy!" Bliss stated before getting out the car. Kiem couldn't help but to grab a nice handful of her soft ass as she got out the car. Before you knew it, Bliss was in the CT6 with the like lights on gliding off into the night. Taking call back streetz until he reached the Holland Tunnel. Kiem shot through the tunnel at a steady pace and breezed uptown. The night life was different in New York, and so was the air. Any official nigga could smell wolves and spot the hounds that lurked the strong streetz of the rotten apple. To a real nigga, same shit different city, but to the weak, it was only the strong that survived. The city stayed lit and it was always something to get into, no matter what time of the day, or night it was. Especially when it came to the bitches, but Kiem understood that a bitch could be a niggaz worst downfall when it came to being in the streetz and getting money. Just knowing he could have damn near any bitch that he came in contact with, was why he stayed loyal, why he stayed committed, and why he respected Bliss the way that he did. It was all too easy for him, and that's what kept him on point like an index finger. Taking in the scenery, he could tell "Angel's" was packed because the entire parking lot was flooded, and the entrance line bent the corner of the building. Pulling through the parking lot entrance, Kiem saw Don Smoke parked to his far left and Gi-Gi's truck parked right next to the R8. He also saw how niggaz was eyeing the Benz as he drove through. trying to see through the tint whose was behind the wheel. He even witnessed the bitches fixin their weave and make up, as he coasts by on the chrome duces. Pulling up slightly pass the clubs entrance, Kiem threw the coupe in reverse and backed up to his left side, right beside Don Smoke. Letting his driver's side window, Don Smoke followed suit and let down his passenger's side window. "Showtime!" Kiem said while taking notice to how sexy Gi-Gi looked sitting in Don's passenger's seat. Blushing hard as ever because she knew Kiem noticed her, but rolling off the molly, she couldn't do nothing but bite down on her lip and drift deep in thought. Feeling so good, her lustful thoughts were interrupted, when Kiem yelled out the window. "Gettt ya hot ass out the car". Him and Don Smoke laughed like crazy, 'cuz they both knew she was in molly world. Reaching in his pocket, Kiem pulled out a fresh stock of blue faces. Immediately tearing the paper band off. he counted out twenty-five blue faces, which was the "K.Y.G." (Keep Ya Gun) fee, plus five hundred extra which was a tip. Then he counted out another fifteen blue faces, to pay for the first fifty ladies waiting in line. Stuffing what was left of the 10 bands back onto his pocket, he rolled up the driver's side window and got out the Benz. With Don Smoke and Gi-Gi both getting out the R8, Don Smoke popped the hood on the Audi which was actually the trunk, and grabbed the Glock camo bucket bag. Making their way towards the club's entrance, Don Smoke and Kiem sandwiched Gi-Gi, as she accompanied them by their arms. To the on lookers that knew the trio that was a hell of a sandwich.

Approaching the entrance, "Big Dream" opened the rope so the squad can gain quick access to the club without waiting into line. Sliding Big Dream twenty five hundred dollars as he dapped him up, Kiem then openly gave him another fifteen hundred, and said to the crowd waiting into line. "The fist fifty ladies y'all come on!" As Don Smoke, Gi-Gi, and himself entered the club, it was crazy how the women bum rushed the entrance, pushing and shoving one another out the way, just to be sure that they made the count. One female even broke a heel and fell, as the others stepped over her racing to gain entrances. It was just one of them nights, and Big Dream seen it happen a thousand times. No matter how cute the ladies were or how phat their asses were, the hood rat always came out of 'em whenever it came to free access. Walking through the club, Kiem instantly witnessed Shark up in V.I.P. with a bunch of TOB'z (Thot Ass Bitches). Looking closer, Kiem noticed every V.I.P. section was full with familiar faces both bitches and niggaz. "Bro, look!" Don Smoke said to Kiem while grabbing him by his shoulder and turning towards their right side. Surprised to see Ms. Estelvo sitting at the bar, Kiem looked at Don Smoke and said, "What she doing up in here?" Both puzzled by Ms. Estelvo's appearance. Don Smoke said, "I don't know! But I'm damn sure 'bout to find out. My nigga look. you and Gi-Gi go play the cut. Stay out of view until I find out what's shaking. Something ain't right!" "I told you that bitch rubs me the wrong way." Don Smoke expressed. Taking Gi-Gi by the hand they slid off deep into the background of the club, still within a good view of the bar. Watching from a distance as Don Smoke walked up to the bar, the bartender served him a double shot of Henny, as she spoke. "Hey Don Smoke!" "What up sexy" he replied. Taking notice how Ms. Estelvo was eyeing him, "give my nigga another round," Nice stated. as he took a seat at the bar and dapped Don Smoke up. "Where bro at?" Nice asked. "He here. Him and Gi-Gi playing the cut right now. But check. you see that foreign bitch sitting with her blouse open to your left." "Yea! She been getting lit since she got here. And she got some perky ass titties too!" Nice replied. "Look tho! The bitch crazy or some shit like that she got a thing for ya bro, plus she owns a condominium complex and who knows what else". "Say word?! So she a rich foreign bitch or maybe she one of them rich foreign bitches that shoot up or snort. Which explains why Nicco kept looking over his shoulder, when they was sitting together 'bout two hours ago!" Nice explained. Red lights starting going off in Don Smoke's head, as he just gained some very important info. Careful not to make anyone aware of the situation like Kiem said, Don Smoke fell right in line and followed up. "Yea the nigga probably was 'noid trying to serve the bitch, thinking she was a set up". Nice and Don Smoke both laughed. "So, where the nigga at now?" Don Smoke asked. "He bounced 'bout forty-five minutes ago, but the nigga is throwing a party at my club next Friday." Nice replied. "Yo! I'm 'bout to go get these bottles and find bro and Gi-Gi, it's almost thunderstorm time. Our table is the one with the purple cloth. I'll be back in a few!" said Nice. Walking towards the back of the club, Nice faded into the crowd. Throwing the second double shot of Henny back, Ms. Estelvo approached Don Smoke. "Hello Don. May I accompany you?" She asked. "Hey Ms. Estelvo. Sure! Nice to see you again!" Don smoke stated. "It's wonderful to see you as well Don." she replied back. "I came out to have a few drinks tonight." Ms. Estelvo stated. "An old friend of mine suggested this place and I've never been one to turn down a good time. However, it is getting late, and I have a few business appointments early tomorrow morning. Uhh where's Mr. Pairings?" Ms. Estelvo asked. "That's a damn good question!" Don Smoke replied. "Haven't heard from him since yesterday, but if I hear anything from him I'll be sure to tell him you inquired about him." "Will you do that for me darling?" Ms. Estelvo asked. "Sure it's no big deal!" Don smoke replied. "Very well then. Give him this message for me as well. Tell him I will be waiting in room 702 at the Double Tree tonight. Tell him it would be very beneficial for him to see me." Ms. Estelvo explained.

She called the bartender over while digging into her Chanel purse and pulling out a wad of cash, "Give this man anything that he wants to drink." as she handed the cash to the bartender. Shaking her lil tight ass as she was exiting the club, Don Smoke wanted to spit on the bitch! He knew she was feeding him a bunch of bullshit. Pulling out his phone he texted Kiem *"Bro.get up here a.s.a.p." "Keep ya fly. this shit is wild but we gone build after Gi-Gi leave."* Feeling his phone vibrate in his pocket twice, Kiem pulled out his phone and seen that Don Smoke sent two texts. Already! He replied. as him and Gi-Gi walked towards the bar, where Don Smoke was sitting. bouncing through the crowd, Nice spotted Kiem and Gi-Gi walking hand and hand, then rolled up on 'em. Y'all make a fly couple! Nice said Jokingly. Yea she mine for life! Kiem replied. as he dapped Nice up. "You look beautiful Gi-Gi!" "Thanks." she told Nice, then hugged him and gave him a kiss on the cheek. "Let's hit our table, Don's waiting for us. Also, bro I checked the club's emails and it did show that Nicco reserved the place for next Friday. So when I asked Tokyo 'bout it she told me that the nigga pulled up on her and gave her thirty thousand cash, which is the rental fee, including 10 free bottles with promotion paid and full. Then he gave her another ten thousand cash, to buy an extra 30 bottles and left her with the thousand dollar tip. But dude didn't want the promotion, that's why I'm just now finding out. And as it checks out the nigga might really be plugged, and if that's the case, we got competition if he's moving at a much better price. The main thing we have on our side is our product being the best shit on the East Coast, well as our clientele. But if this mutha fucka got product as good as ours for the low, we definitely gone have issues." "My nigga. it ain't gone be no issues!" Kiem stated confidently. "Let that nigga do him, all he wanna do is stunt. That nigga don't know money." Gi-Gi, Nice, and Kiem laughed, but on the inside, Kiem was burning hot. This is why he was such a threat, 'cuz he would remain calm and never expose his anger. Especially when it was murder. Back in the presence of Don Smoke, everybody took a seat at the table as the waitress bought over eight bottles and one flute. Everyone grabbed two bottles each and raised them in the air as they all stood back on their feet, as Don Smoke did the honors. "To us, L.F.M. (Loyalty, Family, and Money)". All eight bottles popped as Don Smoke, Kiem, and Nice sipped from each of their bottles. While Gi-Gi poured from reach one of her bottles into the flute, filling it to the rim. Gi-Gi knew the rules, and she knew it wasn't lady like to drink from the bottle unless it was going down, and she was 'bout to beat a bitch ass, or in some cases, a niggaz ass.

The atmosphere was smooth and the clubs vibe was on chill, as DJ EatDaDick played nothing but club bangers. She was one of the most selected few of female DJs to travel the Tri-State's major clubs, and do what she do. Her name was self explanatory 'cuz once upon a time, she too was a pole vixen. French Montana's "Pop That" blasted through the club's speakers as the strippers took stage. "The Latin Power Playas" came out and went straight to work. Marissa Caliente, Backshot Bella, Virgo Supawet, and Punanni Cre`me were four of the baddest Puerto Rican strippers in the game. They knew that their pussy was power over most niggaz who they just played. That's how the group got their name. Don Smoke dumped the bucket bag onto their table, showcasing nothing but racks. As excitement grew in his pants, The Latin Power Playas went crazy! Backshot Bella gave Don Smoke a lap dance reverse cowgirl style, then reversed the position and smuggled his face with her 36 DDD's. Punanni Cre`me bust it open for Kiem, making her pussy pop doing a handstand. Virgo Supawet was grinding so hard on Nice, it looked like they were fucking from a distance. Marissa Caliente took Gi-Gi by the hand and escorted her up on stage, as the crowd went crazy. Still rolling off the Molly, Gi-Gi grabbed the pole and did her down thing, as Marissa Caliente joined in. Feeling herself as she locked eyes with Kiem. Gi-Gi got down one her knees and slowly licked the pole from its base, until she was standing toll. Dollars came from every direction, as the crowd starting chanting, 'take it off, take it off". Fully dressed, Gi-Gi had the spot light, as she unbuttoned her sheer blouse, and flashed the crowd her beautiful plump melons. Bending over so she could position her ass between the pole. The dollars didn't stop coming. Reaching under her mini skirt, she pulled off her black silk panties and tossed 'em off the stage to Kiem. Amazed as he caught her panties, Kiem, Don Smoke, and Nice, all grabbed two stocks of Jacksons and threw it on stage to Gi-Gi, still in the paper band. The crowd grew enormous and clapped out of control, while Gi-Gi picked the money up and joined the fellas back at the table. "I didn't know you got down Ma!" Kiem stated. "I don't. I just wanted to put on for you!" Gi-Gi replied. Tucking the panties into his jacket pocket, Kiem started ripping the paper bands from the money, as Don Smoke and Nice did the same. Shark approached their table and spoke as everyone nodded their head in returned. "I see y'all got this mutha fucka lit. Y'all throwing 5's. I need to get with the program!" Shark stated. "You got ya own." Don Smoke replied. "V.I.P. on smash, bitches everywhere, ya killers posted up! And I hear ya man's doing it big at Main Event next Friday." Don Smoke said sarcastically. "Yea! Yea! He put me on". Shark stated. "He was here earlier, left out tho. He was with some type of foreign bitch. Could tell she was older 'cuz her hands didn't match her face. I guess it's that botox money, but the bitch had some perfect tits." Shark replied. Soaking in all the information with what he just witnessed with his own eyes, Kiem had to find out what the connection was between Ms. Estelvo and Nicco. With all the strippers on the floor, the squad made it thunderstorm while niggaz looked on from the crowd with jealousy in their eyes. Kiem, Don Smoke, and Nice literally changed the game from making it rain to making it thunderstorm. So much money was flyin' into the air and landing on stage, that some of the strippers had to grab brooms to sweep the money up. This was all part of Kiem's plan. "to show no signs of defeat yet conquer and kill". Time was flying and it was now time for the main attraction of the night. The 6 foot Amazon named Treasure took stage, and made her body shake like a salt shaker. Looking at Nice the whole time as she performed, she stood on her right tip toes and threw her left leg behind her head. Slowly spinning around on one leg, she took a rainbow colored candy cane and began penetrating herself. With every inch of the candy cane deep inside of her, the crowd got silent as she spun from her right leg and onto her right knee. Removing her left leg from behind her head, she then spun onto her back as another stripper came on stage and stood beside her holding a ruler. Laying on her back with her legs spread wide open, Treasure made the candy cane shoot out of her pussy into the air, while the second stripper that was holding the ruler caught it and began sucking on it. The crowd went ape shit, fascinated by the performance. Playin'

Coffee 1880 from the wall bar. Don poured Kiem then himself a drink and got down to business. "Bro I know you was viewing things from a distance when Ms. Estelvo approached me, she asked if she could sit with me. I gave her the green light to see how far she was gone take things. She went on to imply that she came out to have a few drinks tonight, because an old friend of hers suggested that place. Now out of every bar, sports bar, and club within the city her friend suggested that spot. It's no coincidence as to why she was there!" Don Smoke stated. "Then Nice even said that she was sitting with Nicco at the bar 'bout 2 hours before we even got there. Said Nicco kept looking over his shoulder like he didn't wanna be seen with the bitch. I made sure not to alert Nice about the situation at hand, just like you said. So once he told me that. I just blended in with the convo, but if you ask me that old friend of hers is Nicco." Don Smoke said through his clenched teeth. "She even asked about your whereabouts. Told her I didn't know, so she asked me to give you a message. Said she'll be waiting in room 702 at the Double Tree tonight and to tell you it will be very beneficial for you to see her." Don Smoke expressed. Pouring himself another drink, Kiem threw it straight back and quickly poured another. "Don that bitch mutha fucka hit my spot!" Kiem stated coldly. "And Ms. Estelvo, I know her freak ass is behind this shit too. It all adds up now!" Kiem stated. "First, Nicco is throwing a party to gain power of position in the streetz being plugged with better prices. Then he's spotted with this domesticated bitch up in one of livest strip clubs in New York. Plus Gi-Gi told me that he offered Pink Bandz 10racks for the pussy. But when she declined his offer, heard he still tossed the bread at her, and told her to clean herself up. That's when he made it known about having the party." Kiem explained. "Hold the fuck up my nigga!" Don Smoke stated in an annoyed tone of voice. "He still gave Pink Bandz ten thousand and told her to clean herself up, after she rejected his jerk ass?" Don Smoke asked. "Yea! My nigga. straight like that!" Kiem stated. "Bro, you know Pink Bandz moms use to work for some escort service, back when Bandz was young. Heard she ran off with like 60k and started banging needles again. A few days later, they found her dead from a hot shot with the needle still stuck in her arm. Word on the street Nicco pops took the contract on her and fixed her. That same night somebody fixed his ass. Shot in the face with a 12 gauge, left him slumped in the middle of the street on Bergen Ave. To this day, the case still cold, but police don't give a fuck! They wanted that rat off the streetz. Then you know Bandz was doing her thing, spinning niggaz for the bread. That'z why the fuck nigga made the comment for her to clean herself up". Don Smoke expressed. "Like mother, like daughter!" Don Smoke stated. "Dammnnn" Kiem said out loud as he poured himself another drink of the Coffee 1880."You gone drown ya self with the cognac, your don't slow down my boyee!"Don Smoke stated. "Mann I need something to balance this rage, and right now the cognac is doing justice." Kiem replied. "But I have to figure out what's the connection between Nicco and Ms. Estelvo. That's the main piece to the puzzle. Anything could be about to happen, and I ain't getting rocked to sleep." Kiem stated. "You don't know the name of Escort Service Bandz moms worked for?" Kiem asked. "Nah.my nigga! I just know it was some top-notch shit. Secret society type shit unless you know somebody in that line of work. The only person that might know is Bandz." Don Smoke answered. "I kinda figured that! But I don't want to erupt any hurt and pain, nor appear disrespectful inquiring about a service her moms worked for." Kiem stated. "I feel you bro. sometimes it's best not to pick at the scab until the wound fully heals". Don Smoke said. "So what you gone do about Ms. Estelvo at the Double Tree?" Don Smoke asked. "Leave her ass right there! It's nothing beneficial for me that she can say or do without wanting something in return." Kiem stated. "I play chess my nigga and I'm nice with it! All that beneficial shit is nothing but a bait tactic to lure me into her presence. We got business to handle, that silicone titty having bitch ain't important!" Kiem stated. "Also, you know that cash you got on deck from the run down in Delaware, plus the other business that you took care of? I want you to keep that for ya self!" Kiem stated. "My nigga. I think you had too many drinks. It's 375k in the safe and you talking 'bout keep it! Yea, you lit my nigga." Don Smoke said. Laughing at the expression on Don Smoke face Kiem managed to say "All jokes aside, keep that cash bro. I'm not drunk! Everything is about to change. The whole squad is about to get richer. The connect hit me with 500 brickz. Plus gave me some cash so I can get back right. I explained what happened and told him that I used every penny of my personal stash to make good on my word with him. He understood my point of view, but most importantly, he respected my loyalty. The rest is history." Kiem explained. "Damn my nigga! I don't even know how to thank you." Don Smoke expressed. " You've done more than enough just being loyal." Kiem replied. "The fall of many great empires come from the lack of loyalty. It's no way Imma be out here winning, and my team not scoring. One rise, we all rise! Somebody fall, hold 'em down! Somebody talk, kill the rat! We can't leave room for no mice, it's that fucking simple!" Kiem stated. "Things here are 'bout to get hot, so we gotta shake and move to keep the heat up off us." "So how soon are we rockin'?" Don Smoke asked. "Like yesterday." Kiem replied. "I got a lot of whipping to do. I'm talking 'bout wrist on steroids! We gone take 100 brickz and triple the weight, all crack! Then we gone take another 100 brickz and double the weight, all coke! With 500 brickz of crack and cocaine combined, we hit the interstate and get rich or catch a case my nigga! Then it's still another 300 brickz for me to get the connect his money and make our own debut." Kiem expressed. "After this run right here, we paying for everything we touch! Fuck that consignment shit. It was gravy while it lasted, but now we buy into the connect. We still get the same grade product in bulk quantity, but at a much lower price. The connect will want our business, just as we will want his, so everybody eats!" Kiem stated. "Let's do it." Don Smoke said. "I'll hit you up tomorrow my nigga. It's damn near 5:00am and knowing Bliss she's up waiting on a nigga making sure I make it home safe!" Kiem stated. "Yea! You know how sis gets. so you need to beat the clock! Don Smoke said as he chuckled. "I know man!" Kiem replied. "One my nigga!" Don Smoke said while dapping Kiem up.

Making the run home thoughts raced through his mind about Ms. Estelvo and Nicco. He had to find out the connection between them. He thought hard but remembered what Don told him about Bandz mom's. "Shit is crazy." he said out loud. Still in thought, he smiled as he pulled into the driveway and parked. "Aunty!" He said out loud. Ai'Adore will most likely know something about Bliss mom's past, and the name of that escort service she worked for. Unlocking the door, he quickly entered the house where

Bliss met him at the door and dragged him into the room, like a lion dragging its prey into its den. Stumbling onto the floor, Bliss got up and stood over top of Kiem and dropped her silk kimono robe. Standing in pure perfection Kiem felt his nature rise as Bliss demanded him to strip. "Strip nigga. I want everything off now!" Playing in her pussy while Kiem submitted to her demand. Her juices ran down her fingers as she squeezed on her nipples with her other hand. Laying on the floor with his dick stiffer than a frozen neck bone, Bliss kneeled down and put her fingers into his mouth, as he tasted her sweet juices. "Ummmmm" she moaned while Kiem licked on her fingers. "It tastes good don't it daddy?" Bliss asked while she reached for his super erect dick and rubbed her thumb over its head in a circular motion. Turned on by her erotic ways, Kiem tried to play with her pussy but she playfully slapped his hands away. Bringing her hand up to her mouth, she spit into her palm then gently started to massage Kiem's manhood. Kissing on his neck, then his lips, and working her way down Kiem knew that Bliss was gone try to make him pay from earlier. But she had another thing coming 'cuz he had a trick up his sleeve as well. Taking all of him into her mouth, Kiem knew that it was on grabbing her by the hair. Kiem talked dirty to her which turned 'em both on, while she performed a miracle. "Suck dis dick like you mean it." Kiem demanded. Saliva dripped from her mouth, as she slurped, sucked, gagged, and deep throated Kiem like her life was on the line! Ummm.ahun.mm!!! Was all Bliss could say awhile satisfying Kiem. Reaching his final destination, Kiem blasted off like a rocket all inside of Bliss mouth and deep down her throat! Careful not to waste a drop as she swallowed every bit. Kiem tried to ease away, but Bliss was having her way with him. Still rocking the mic, she started playing with Kiem's balls, as she instantly felt him grow fully erect inside her mouth again. Going crazy from her handle on him, he knew he couldn't top out. Reaching into his pocket, he pulled out a gram of Molly, all without Bliss knowing because she was so deep into her performance, that she didn't notice him reaching. Throwing the whole gram of Molly into his mouth, Kiem instantly felt it's effect as he started to get hot and sweat! All The Way Up!!! Was now how Kiem was feeling. "Bliss ass was in serious shit now.he thought to himself,as he now performed. "Get ya sexy ass over here" Kiem said as he snatched her by the hair and started kissing and sucking on her breasts! Running two fingers up inside her, as his thumb massaged her clit, she went crazy trying to get away. Feeling like He-Man on some savage sex shit, Kiem licked and kissed all over her stomach, around her waistline, working his way down to her thighs. Moaning and gasping for air. Bliss felt sensations run through her body like never before. "Ooh bae! Damnn! Ahhh! Yea.right there! Ooohhh.oohhh! Kiem went to work like a fat person at an all you can eat buffet the way he sucked, licked, nibbled, and kissed on her clit bringing her to the point of ecstasy. Bliss's body shook and trembled as she came all over Kiem's tongue and face, while holding him by his ears. "I love you daddy! I love you soooo fucking much." she said as her eyes started tearing up. Pushing Kiem down onto his back, she straddled him then placed his pipeline inside of her, as she clawed his chest going up and down in a steady rhythm. Grabbing her by her ass, Kiem met her rhythm and pumped up into her, every time she came down on him. Looking into his eyes she made her hips do all the work while her juices ran down his pipe. With Versace on the floor, Bliss already had it in her mind that this was where she wanted to please Kiem. Bouncing up and down she arched her back deep and came all over Kiem's dick. Soaked with her juices, Kiem took bliss by the hand and led her over to the bed and bent her over. Eating her candy from the back, he wanted to make sure she was nice and wet before he dig her back out. "Get ya ass up on the bed and get on all fours" Kiem demanded." Bliss did as she was told. She pulled the silk Versace linen back and told Kiem "I always wanted to get fucked on a million dollars." Positioned on all four while looking back at Kiem, he penetrated her long and deep! "Ahhhh!! Daddy. daddy!! fuck dis pussy. fucckkk!! Baaeee.bae wait!! Wait.ahhhhh waiitttt!!! It hurts. it hurts soooo good!" Turned on by Bliss's reactions, Kiem continued pounding her out. Holding her by the waist so she couldn't run Kiem said to her,"this pussy is awesome!" As she said to him "I want to feel ya hot cum inside me!" With a few deep strokes Bliss backed her ass up into Kiem as he came long and hard all up inside of her. Exhausted from such a workout they just laid there breathing heavily, while Kiem held Bliss from the back. With his dick still hard poking her in the ass, Bliss said to him. "I see somebody's still up, you must've really been horny". "Yea for this supa soaker." Kiem replied. "Awweee!!" Bliss said then turned over, snuggled closer to him and drifted off to sleep.

Fresh out the bathtub, Bliss was sore from earlier this morning. She never experienced such a pounding in her life, and the way Kiem mauled her from the back, made her insides tickle. Scrambling a few eggs, she opened a box of turkey sausage links and put them into the skillet. With the buttered toast on a plate and strawberry jam and butter, Bliss added some scrambled eggs, and sausage links, then grabbed a container of bright and early out the fridge, and headed back to the bedroom. With the smell of breakfast in the air, Kiem tossed and turned as Bliss kissed him on the lips. "Morning Sunshine", she said.as he sat up in bed and said good morning back. "Oh! You cooked?!" Kiem said sarcastically. "After the way you ate those groceries early this morning. shiittt,the least I could do is feed you!" Bliss replied. Getting back into bed, she snuggled up under Kiem and watched him eat. "Ma I need you to facetime Ai'Adore for me." Kiem stated. "Something wrong?" Bliss asked. "Nah never that! I just need her to fill me in on some things if she's able to do so." Kiem replied. "Found out some major shit last night. Just need to figure out the connection between Nicco and Ms. Estelvo now!" Kiem stated. "Okay bae! I'm 'bout to hit her now." Bliss said. "Hey Aunty!" Bliss said happily as Ai'Adore answered. "How you been baby?" Ai'Adore asked. "I'm good and you?" Bliss replied. "You know I'm getting it like usual!" Ai'Adore replied." And you can take your head from underneath the covers Kiem." Ai'Adore stated. "What up Ai'Adore?" Kiem asked. "You" she replied back! "I see y'all two been up since early this morning! Who topped out first?" Ai'Adore playfully asked as she laughed. "Aunty I need your help with something." Kiem said. "If I'm able to help you, you know that I will." Ai'Adore stated. "Listen, did you know Pink Bandz mother?" Kiem asked. "Unique? Of course I knew her. She was a real sweetheart! Sad that she died the way that she did, but you know Karma is a mutha fucka!" Ai'Adore expressed. "The asshole that's responsible for her death ended up getting his face blown off that same night." Ai'Adore stated. "Did you know the name of the escort service where she worked?" Kiem asked. Looking like she just seen a ghost, Ai'Adore was stunned by the question. "Excuse me Kiem?" she said as she took a minute to gather herself. Taking a deep breath, she said "the name of the escort service was called Hammer Time." Ai'Adore explained. "It was owned by this Russian bitch named Karma Estelvo. She has very strong Russian Mobb ties and is wealthier than one can imagine. I'm talking about a couple of billion, and she owns property all across the states." Ai'Adore explained. "Why is it that you inquire about Unique?" Ai'Adore asked. "I was trying to find out the connection between Ms. Karma Estelvo and this bitch nigga named Nicco." Kiem stated. "You talking about Nicholas son little Nick?" Ai'Adore asked. "Word has it that it was him who gave Unique that bad fix, all for a few coins. And it's a shame because we all used to work for that same escort service, Unique. myself, and Joany, little Nick's mother." Ai'Adore expressed. "I had to part ways 'cuz the bitch is ruthless and deceitful! She's into everything in the underground market. Her biggest venture is sex trafficking and human trafficking! She has authorities on the payroll, cops, judges, prosecutors all that type of shit. This is a bitch that buys and manipulates her way through life. Bottom line, she's dangerous Kiem." Ai'Adore stated. "She felt sorry for little Nick after his father was killed because she knew that she put the hit out on him and being that her company no longer desired the services of Joany. Karma left her with a bad crack habit. To keep her mouth closed about everything she seen and heard, Karma would give little Nick money to buy work from niggaz in big quantity so he can profit and also supply his mother's habit. Are you in some kind of trouble nephew?" Ai'Adore asked. "Nah aunty! I just needed to put this puzzle together. My condo was broken into. 750k plus 100 brickz gone! No one knew that was a stash house. Not even Bliss. Then all of a sudden, Nicco is throwing a party at Main Event, and he supposed to be plugged with better prices. Then he's seen with Ms. Estelvo up in the strip club. But to make shit worse, the condo that I bought sits on property owned by Ms. Estelvo." Kiem stated. "You don't suppose she had something to do with your place being robbed, do you??" Ai'Adore asked. "At first, I didn't know who, what, when, where, or how! But after all the information I've gathered, I know that she had something to do with it. The job was too clean. The safe was completely drilled opened!" Kiem stated. "But why would she want to rip you off when the bitch is beyond wealthy?" Ai'Adore asked." That's the part I can't figure out.". Kiem stated. "Be honest. Have you ever had any run ins with Karma? Like did she ever try to flirt with you, give you things, or pursue you?" Ai'Adore asked. "I mean she mysteriously popped up on me out of nowhere one day when I just got finished serving Nicco. Then she gave me a watch, 'cuz she said I looked like a man that demanded respect and she had such the gift to accommodate my style." Kiem said. "Let me guess. The watch was a Rainbow-Bezel Rose Gold Daytona." Ai'Adore said. "How'd you know?" Kiem asked. "Boy!! This crazy bitch been eyeing you for at least two years. The watch was a custom order from a friend of mine down in Florida. She told me that she had met a handsome young man whom she had grown quite fond of and wanted to give him a wonderful birthday gift. She asked me if I can have the watch delivered to her as soon as possible!" Ai'Adore explained. "Usually it's a two to three year waiting period for that kind of custom Rolex, but for a few extra thousand any jeweler will fill the order!" Ai'Adore stated. Steaming hot, Bliss rolled her eyes at Kiem and said,"Oh bitches buying you roleys now?! What this Russian bitch think I won't spin on her rich ass!" Bliss angrily said. "It's nothing like that Ma. Calm ya ass down!" Kiem stated. "Shit is bigger than what it seems!" Kiem stated. "He's right Bliss!" Ai'Adore explained. "This bitch will stop at nothing until she gets what she wants. And from the look of things Kiem is what she wants!" "One last question. is that escort service still up and running?" Kiem asked. "It is. Only difference now is that she operates out of New Haven, Ct. It's more discreet for her to do business out there." Ai'Adore stated. "But this woman is poison Kiem and she has her eyes set on you,so she will go beyond extreme measures to have hold of you! You might want to consider avoiding all contact with her. And before I go I want you to know that Unique never ran off with no money as word has it on the streetz!! That bitch Karma wanted her daughter to become a worker because of her beauty and how developed her body was to only be 13. She knew old, lonely, desperate men would pay as much as $75,000 to $100,000 for a few minutes with her, but when Unique refused to give her daughter up, Karma offered her 60 thousand. Unique threatened to go the FBI about everything if she even looked at her daughter wrong. Feeling over powered and threatened by Unique going to the FBI she placed a contract on her head." Ai'Adore said tearfully. "Look aunty I greatly appreciate ya help. I'm gonna handle things before shit gets out of hand!" Kiem stated. "And you make sure you let me know anything, I mean anything. if it concerns me, Bliss, or anybody in my squad!!" Kiem said harshly. "Guess I holla at y'all. love you Bliss and you too Kiem!" Ai'Adore said. "We love you too aunty." Bliss replied back before they ended the call. "This shit is surreal. The whole time I've been living in that condo, the bitch been eyeing me. Clocking my every move. But I don't understand why she got it bad for me and she knows that you're my woman! I made that known when we went to go look at the place together." Kiem expressed. "Better believe she knows I'm yours daddy!" Bliss stated. "'Cuz if the bitch don't…that's her ass Mr. Postman!!! And I'm sooo fucking serious right now!" Bliss said harshly. "Calm down killer." Kiem said with a slight chuckle. "You damn right I will kill when it comes to you. Loyalty is all I know." Bliss stated coldly. Looking deep into her eyes Kiem felt every word that Bliss said deep within his veins. He knew that she loved him unconditionally, and he loved her just the same! Pulling Bliss into his arms, he held her tight knowing that their energy was one and the same. He also knew that he had to make moves, well as put the brickz up that was still in his trunk. With his hind parts starting to grow numb from laying and sitting on stacks of blue faces all morning long Kiem got up and started stretching to relieve his backside. Looking at the money scattered all over the bed, Kiem noticed that a few of the paper bands had popped loose from the money during their wee hour extravaganza! Still in the nude laying across the money, Bliss looked at Kiem and laughed. Kiem tried to figure out what was so funny that he had to ask "What you take a laughing pill, or some shit? What's so funny??" Come here bae. Turn around and look in the mirror! Bliss asked of Kiem. Doing as she asked Bliss peeled off the three hundred dollar bills that was stuck to his ass. "Yea! My nigga a real money maker!" Bliss said jokingly. Then stuck her tongue in his ear and whispered. "Yea! Dis that sticky fly trap". Shaking his head. Kiem

opened it. Placing the kilos inside he then went back into the bedroom and collected all of the cash off of the bed. With all the money inside the 3-D monogram bag, he went back into the bathroom and began stocking the money inside the safe. With everything neatly stocked he kept 100k in the bag, which would be money for traveling expenses! After positioning the bathtub back in its proper place, he went back into the bedroom and waited for Bliss to finish getting herself together. Entering the bedroom looking like she just came back from a Gucci fashion show, Kiem stood amazed at how beautiful she was. Smiling because she knew Kiem thought highly of her and it made her feel spectacular! "Well, I got to run a few errands. You know, pick up a few things for the house and do a lil shopping." Bliss stated. Reaching into the bag, Kiem took out a paper banned stock of blue faces and handed it to Bliss. "I got money bae, plus you left like six thousand in ya jeans pocket." Bliss said. "Well now you got more!" Kiem stated. "Ma listen! Me and Don Smoke 'bout to make a few moves out of state. We rocking tonight, but we'll be back in a few days. Just gotta open shop in a few different spots. It's 'bout to be blazing here. So out of sight, out of mind!" "I understand Kiem. Ya ass just need to make sure that you understand I'm here waiting for you!" Bliss stated. Feeling her point of view Kiem thought about how she'd be worried to death about him knowing that anything could take place with him being hundreds of miles away from home. Kissing her on the lips, he pulled her close and caressed her face! Staring in her eyes he ran his fingers through her long wavy hair to reassure her that he'd make it back to her safe. Bliss hugged him so tight that he could actually feel her heartbeat! To Kiem it was one of those beautiful moments. Holding Bliss by her hand, and the 3-D monogram bag in the other they both walked downstairs to the garage! Opening his driver's side back door Kiem grabbed the two laundry sacks off the floor and put it the duffle bag then put the bag into the trunk. Bliss activated the house alarm then got inside the car with Kiem. Once the garage door opened the Cadillac eased through and stopped right beside the Benz, as the garage door closed! Bliss kissed Kiem passionately on the lips before getting out the car and getting into her own. Watching as she got in the Benz, Kiem waited for her to start the car and pull out of the driveway, as he tailed behind. After going in separate directions, Kiem hit Don Smoke on speed dial. "What's shaking my nigga?" Don Smoke asked as he answered the phone. "I'm in rotation!" Kiem replied. "My nigga! I caught wave of everything that was missing. This shit is bazaar! But I have to send a message. I can't slip up dealing with this foreign bitch." Kiem expressed. "I told you that bitch wasn't right! Just couldn't put my finger on it as to why." Don Smoke stated. "Yeah you definitely called it my nigga." Kiem said. "Don look I'm 'bout to hit Pink Bandz right quick. She's gone need to make this run with us! I'll be pulling up in 'bout 20 minutes then I'll pour you the full drink." Kiem stated. "Kool my nigga! I'll catch you when you get here." Don Smoke replied. After their lines went dead Kiem thought about the process of explaining everything as he hit Pink Bandz on speed dial. Laying on her couch relaxing Bandz phone started ringing back to back. As she reached for it, she saw Kiem's name flash across the caller display. "Kiem! What's mobbin' nigga?" Bandz asked. "You, me, us, the squad!" Kiem replied. "Yo you dressed ma?" Kiem asked. "If you call a pair of boy shorts and a cami dressed then yea!" Bandz replied. "That's straight we'll go shopping and get whatever you want! But I need you to come right now! I'm gone need you to make a run with me and Don Smoke. Plus I need to build with you face to face 'bout some very important shit! I believe that you've been searching for the truth long enough now it's time to serve justice." Kiem explained. "What da fuck u talkin' 'bout boyee?" Bandz asked. "Trust me on this I've NEVER misled you, nor guided you in the wrong direction. I've been nothing but loyal and truthful with you since day one!" Kiem stated. "You right! I can't say nothin foul 'bout u, not even if I wanted too, but I'm definitely with da run. Da shoppin' too!" Bandz giggled. "Ma! Leave ya truck parked where it's at and catch an Uber to Don Smoke spot now! I'll be waiting on you!" Kiem said. "Let me throw on my 95 air max and grab my purse and I'm on my way." Bandz stated.

Pulling up outside of Don Smoke's apartment building Kiem quickly parked the car, then jumped out and hurried into the building. Soon as he got upstairs, Don Smoke greeted him at the door then passed him the backwood. "I need to burn this!" Kiem stated as he entered the apartment pulling on the back wood. Taking a seat on the sofa, Don Smoke poured two shots of Deau Black Cognac. then took a seat opposite from Kiem. Handing Kiem his drink, Kiem exchanged hands passing Don the back wood with one and taking the drink with the other. "Good look bro!" Kiem said then took a sip of the cognac. "Wooo!! This shit hits hard, but it releases intense floral flavors." Kiem said after hitting the cognac. "Yea! This shit here is a blend of Grande Champagne and Petite Champagne cognacs." Don Smoke replied. "But it's definitely worth the MSRP." Don Smoke stated. "My nigga! Check this ill shit!" Kiem expressed. "Remember when you said unless I know somebody that was in that line of work. Bandz would be the only person that might be able to fill me in on the name of the escort service where her moms worked? Well my nigga!! It just so happens that I did know someone, Bliss's aunt, Ai'Adore. I racked my fucking brain on the way home, tryna figure out someone that I knew, but it wasn't until I pulled into my driveway that she popped into my head. So I had Bliss hit her for me then I got right to the point. The story goes like this. Her moms name was Unique and everyone I mean everyone loved her. The mutha fucka responsible for her death got his face blown off that same night. The name of the escort service she worked for is called "Hammer Time". It's owned by this Russian bitch named none other than Karma Estelvo." "What the fuck!!!!?" Don Smoke surprisingly stated. "The bitch has very strong Russian mobb ties and she's worth more than we both can imagine. A couple of Billion to be exact. Word has it that it was Nicco's father who gave Bandz moms that bad fix. They all use to work together for that same escort service. Unique, Ai'Adore, and Joany, Nicco's mom. Ai'Adore said she parted ways because the bitch is ruthless! She also has authorities on the payroll. Claims she felt sorry for Nicco after his father was killed, because she knew that she put the hit out on him. After her company no longer desired the services of Nicco's moms, Ms. Estelvo left her with a bad crack habit, which left her vulnerable and dependent. So to keep her mouth closed about everything, Ms. Estelvo would give Nicco money to buy work in huge quantities." Kiem carefully explained. "Ai'Adore is the one that ordered the Rolex from a friend of hers down in Florida. The bitch told her some bullshit about how she met a young man and wanted to give him a wonderful birthday gift. Ai'Adore said that the bitch will stop at nothing until she gets what she wants! And from the look of things what she wants is me! The escort service is still up and running. She operates out of New Haven, CT now. Looks like she has her eyes set on me and will go beyond extreme measures to have hold of me. Bandz moms never ran off with no money. That was all bullshit. Ms. Estelvo wanted Bandz to become a worker within her sex trafficking ring, but when Bandz moms refused to give her up Ms. Estelvo offered her 60k, so Bandz moms threatened to go to the FBI about everything if the bitch even looked at her daughter wrong. She felt overpowered and threatened by Bandz moms going to the FBI, so she placed a contract on her head. Not to mention that the bitch been watching me, and clocking my every move the whole 2years that I've been living in that condo." Kiem stated. "Man I can hardly believe this shit." Don Smoke replied. "Tell me about it!" Kiem said. "It's too ugly now to go pussy. Too much money was taken from me and now I have to make a statement!" Kiem said non remorseful!

Hearing a light knock at the door Don Smoke said to Kiem, "That must be Bandz!" Bandz entered the apartment and made both Kiem and Don Smoke's mouths drop!! Standing there in a pair of lime green booty shorts, with a silver and grey cami and a pair of sliver, grey, and lime green 95 air max made her look victorious! "Give me some love niggaz!" Bandz said. "Y'all actin' like u neva seen a phat pussy, a phat ass, and the titties to go with it!" Bandz stated while smiling. "Not like that!" Don Smoke said jokingly while giving her a hug. "And what I got to get ass naked to get some love?" She playfully asked Kiem. "Ma ya ass off the meter. You know you gets nothing but love from the guy!!" Kiem said as he gave her a big hug. "Fire that shit up niggaz we 'bout to get lit and move on these streetz!!" Bandz said excitedly. "So what u have to build with me about?" Bandz asked Kiem. Looking frustrated Kiem replied, "I'm gone holla at you when we get to where we going. This shit is business." "Say nothin more!" Bandz replied. As she took a seat on the sofa next to Kiem handing her a glass with one ice cube inside, Don Smoke poured her a shot of Deau Black Cognac. Taking a sip. "Ahhh!! Dis shit here is pure truth!" Bandz said as she began licking her bottom lip. "It's crazy when you first taste it but it's unexplainable after. I likez dis!" Bandz expressed. Taking a pack of 1882 blunts out of her purse, Bandz emptied the guts out of one inside the astray and started stuffing it with 2.5 of Pineapple kush. Lighting the blunt up, Bandz hit it three times then passed it to Don Smoke. Don Smoke followed suit then passed it to Kiem. With the blunt in full rotation, Don Smoke quickly retrieved a pound of Raspberry Pomegranate Kush! This was a personal strand of weed his California connect sent him. Don could get his hands on weed, most niggaz never even heard of. Don was a lock to get blessed with finest of the finest when it came to marijuana. Inhaling the savory aroma as she held the weed up to her face, Bandz tore through the plastic and took a handful of the raspberry pomegranate kush. and began breaking it up on the table. "Dammmnnn!!! Dis shit smells like it's killa!" Bandz stated. "Da budz are like nothin I've ever seen before. This shit is fluffier than cotton candy and softer than my ass!!!" Bandz stated. "Now that I seriously doubt! You could stuff ya ass inside a pillowcase, then drop it on some pins and needles and won't feel a pinch! Now it gets no softer than that!!" Kiem said jokingly. "Boyee u stupiiddd!!!" Bandz replied while Don Smoke laughed his ass off twisting another 1882 this time with the RPK(Raspberry Pomegranate Kush). Bandz fired up and immediately starting choking off its potent smoke. "Oh! This weed here. This that Exxon. This shit got me feelin' supa!" Bandz said. "Well pass that so we can feel supa too!" Don Smoke stated. Pulling on the blunt he started choking off the smoke instantly. Time was flying and the plan was to move out at late noon but it was now almost 4:00 pm. Don Smoke got up and grabbed the guns that was togging along for the run! Laying the weapons on the table, Bandz clutched the Para Ordance 1911 40 S&W, and said "I like this! This bitch here gone learn a nigga! And I got 30 for that ass!" This is another reason why Kiem chose her to make the run with him and Don Smoke, she was always ready for gunplay. Wrapping the Glock 22, the Glock 21, and the 40 S&W inside a beach towel, Don Smoke then grabbed 3 boxes of F&N bullets, and put them inside a small paper bag and placed it on top of the towel. With the extendos loaded for each gun, the squad was ready to hit the interstate. Stuffing the pound of weed inside a vacuum sealed zip lock, Kiem tucked it under his shirt and exited the apartment. Kiem tossed Bandz his smart key and told her to drive. Getting into the R8 with Don Smoke, Kiem handed him the weed then told him to go to the house in New Castle. "I'll catch you when you get there!" They dapped each other up then Kiem got out the car and got into his." You took long enough." Bandz said to Kiem. "Gotta make sure my nigga good before anything!" Kiem replied. "I know. Just fuckin with ya." Bandz said. Don Smoke put the code in so that the floor compartment could eject and then he placed the towel and small paper bag inside before pulling off. Adjusting the driver's seat Bandz put on her seat belt and pushed the CT6 with ease. "Ma, it's 200 brickz in the trunk, watch ya speed when we get on the turnpike. Make sure you do the speed limit. Nothing more nothing less!" Kiem stated. "I got you nigga! Chillax and let ya nuts hang! I know dem trooperz b in da cut, waitin' fa a mutha fucka! Fuck 'em!" Bandz said aggressively. "This is why I fuckz with u Kiem. You stay on ya shit, while these decoyz are just that...decoyz!" Bandz genuinely said. "Thanks for the love ma! I genuinely fucks with you too!" Kiem stated. "Nigga stop! U gone make a bitch pussy wet with ya sensitive thug ass!" Bandz said to Kiem. "You ill ma! Ya ass stay with a comeback for everything." Kiem stated. "I'm that bitch what more can I say!" Bandz replied. "Seriously though, we got some business to handle!" Kiem stated and then continued. "I'm gone need for you to hold ya self together. This is a mind over matter situation, and we can't just ride off our anger. Feel me?" Kiem asked. "I'm not trying to cause no type of hurt or pain, but do you remember anything about ya moms past? Like who she use to work for, the name of the company, or anything like that?" Kiem asked. Ignoring his question Kiem could tell that she was feeling some type of way. After driving in silence for almost an hour, Bandz started talking. "Kiem what's up? Why u askin' me shit ' bout my dead mother? What you know somethin' I don't nigga?" Bandz asked. "Listen Ma! I need you to tell me anything that you know or might remember. This is where we bond for real! You know I would never bring up ya past if it wasn't important!" Kiem stated. "Why?!" She yelled out loud as tears started talking running down her face. Trying to get herself together, she began trying to talk. "I. I remember at she use to work for some foreign woman. Could tell she wasn't from da States by her accent. The bitch use to always look at me like she wanted me, ya kno! I was young so a lot of shit I was blind to you know?! But I can neva forget the name of that place she worked. It was called "Hammer Time." All I heard after my momz died was that she ran off with some money. It's nothin' else I recall 'bout that place!" Bandz tearfully explained. "Oh wait Kiem!" Bandz said excitedly. "The bitch use to keep a lot of money in the office wall safe in the back! And this Chinese woman that works the front desk was the only one who knows the combo besidez that foreign bitch!" Bandz stated. "I use to watch her put stockz and stockz of money inside while I was playin' with my Barbies and shit!" Bandz said. "Ma! I know the whole truth about what happened to ya mother!" Kiem stated. "I just found out a whole bunch of shit within a matter of days." Kiem said. "Your moms was murdered. That same foreign bitch you talking 'bout, is the one who put a contract out on ya mother. Word got 'round on the streetz that she ran off with 60k from that escort service, but that's not what happened. Your mother was murdered trying to protect you! That foreign bitch wanted you to become a worker. When ya moms refused to give you up that bitch whose name is Karma Estelvo offered ya moms 60k. Ya moms still refused and threatened to go to the FBI 'bout everything. So in turn Karma put out a contract on her." Kiem explained. "But check it! Nicco's pops is the one that took the contract. His name was Nicholas and that same night he gave ya moms that bad fix, he got killed too. Karma put a hit out on him as well. The bitch is ruthless, and she has strong Russian Mobb ties as well as 12, judges, lawyers, and prosecutors on the payroll." "Dammnnn nigga! This bitch sounds like she's a one man wreckin' crew!" Bandz stated. "At least I know what I'm up against. My name is everything out here, and that bitch is going to pay! Nicco is going to pay and his mother and whoever else gets in my fucking way is going to pay!" Kiem stated harshly! "Bandz my condo was broken into and 750k and 100 brickz was taken. The condo I bought sits on property that's owned by Karma, so the whole two years I've been living there, she been watching me and clocking my every move! No one knew that my condo was a safe house, not even Bliss! And the only one besides me that knew about the safe, is the company that installed it. Nicco is the one who hit my spot. That's the reason he's plugged now and running around spending all this money! I don't even know that he even knows it was my spot he hit. That 10k he offered you to fuck, where you think he got that kind of money from? Kiem asked. When you denied him and he still tossed the money at you and said clean ya self up, he was just being sarcastic. He was referring to ya moms knowing she used to work for an escort service, and how you use to play niggaz for the money. So in his eyes like mother, like daughter!" Kiem stated. "Am I making any sense?" Kiem asked Bandz. "Nigga u just made all da sense and I've always searched fa da truth. but kept gettin' nowhere. Now that I have it it's time for me to slide on some shit!" Bandz said. "No one is to know anything about this conversation! No one." Kiem said seriously. "Once we get where we going, me and you are gonna go pay Joany a farewell visit!" Kiem stated harshly. "Who the fuck is Joany?" Bandz asked. "It's that bitch nigga Nicco's mom!" Kiem replied. That's what da fuck I'm talkin' 'bout Kiem! Kill.kill.murda,murda! Bandz said in a arrogant, but stern tone of voice.Can I ask u something Kiem? Bandz asked. Sure Ma! Kiem replied. How'd u find out 'bout things because you just don't know the burden that was lifted off my shoulders. My mother gave her life to protect her only child and it's no fuckin' way I'm lettin' dis shit ride! I'm slidin' on every opp! That's on God nigga!" Bandz angrily expressed. Kiem looked at her and knew that she had a lot of built up anger and frustration deep inside of her. At some point she had to let it out before it destroyed her. Rubbing her shoulder, Kiem told her things were going to be alright. He understood her pain because he lost his mother to cardiac arrest, while he was doing a bid. So it's things that still bothered him as well, and this is why he was able to relate. Bandz quickly glanced back at Kiem and stated "Thingz are gone be alright huh?!" "You know that they are Ma! You have to believe. You've come too far in life, for things not to!" Kiem explained. "Kiem you a real down to earth nigga! Ur actually da first nigga that I've eva met that's just all around everything, that every woman wants in a man!" Bandz expressed. "Thanks!" Kiem replied slightly blushing. "Don't thank me! Thank your momma for your respect and mannerisms and thank your daddy for your Gangsta!" Bandz stated. "You're something else Bandz. You're very unique!" Kiem replied. Tears streamed down her face as she tried to hold them back! "Let it out Ma. Let it out!" Kiem said to her as he wiped her tears with the back of his hand. "Do you even know that my birth name is Unique?" Bandz asked Kiem. "Huh??!! I thought that your name was Mecca." Kiem replied. "No crazy! Mecca is my middle name. I've always felt like my mother abandoned me for drugs, and I was so ashamed cuz of her addiction and her lifestyle that I just always went by my middle name! My name is actually "Unique Mecca". I feel so fucked up now knowin' that my moms never gave up on me!" Bandz expressed. "Sometimes it be like that Ma! One thing ' bout the truth, you can't dilute it! That's why time is the biggest snitch! In due time all things reveal itself." Kiem explained. But I love your name. It's very powerful with purpose!" Kiem stated. "Thankz nigga!" Bandz said to Kiem as she started smiling. "You're more than welcome Ma! It's my responsibility to make sure that all of my ladies are straight!" Kiem stated. "Okay playa!" Bandz said sarcastically. "Nah Ma! Never a playa just a nigga that cares!" Kiem replied. The Galaxy whistled as Kiem grabbed his phone from the center console. Going to his messages Kiem saw Don Smoke's text which read "Here. everything straight?" "Already! Be there in like 25mins or less". Kiem replied back. "Take the exit to ya left and turn right at the light, when you get to the end of the ramp." Kiem told Bandz.

Pulling up in front of their out of state destination, Bandz put the car in reverse and backed up the driveway and into the garage. Instantly. the sensors automatically closed the garage door and locked, once the vehicle was inside. The smell of weed was in the air and hit Bandz and Kiem's nostrils hard as hell as Don Smoke came downstairs into the garage, burning a backwood. Rushing out from behind the steering wheel. "Move boy. I gotta pee", Bandz stated as she bumped into Don Smoke almost knocking him over. "Slow down Ma 'fore you run into the wall!" Don Smoke told Bandz as she zoomed by him. Opening the trunk Kiem grabbed two of the laundry sacks as Don Smoke snatched up the duffle bag. Once in the den, Don Smoke passed the backwood to Kiem as they sat to start counting. Bandz entered the den as Kiem passed her the backwood. "Damnnn! Y'all move quick. All a bitch did was pee and wipe down!" Bandz stated. "You good Ma! Handle ya business. Most females would just use the bathroom then pull their panties back up. No wipe down, no washing the hands, no nothing!" Kiem

the corner top of if off and used it for a scoop. Sniff. sniff. snifff! Snifff! As Bo$$ sunk down low in the driver's seat feeling the effects of the heroin. Bo$$ drifted off in deep thought, thinking about how this job will pay off big for him! He can then pay Smooth off cuz he owed the nigga on the low, from developing a dope habit. Smooth was one of Brick City's finest. A big dawg that had the Weequahic Section on smash with the Heroin. His whole team had that bag and it was nothing to get Bo$$ out the way. Bo$$ himself, even knew that as well, but as long as he kept his habit in the dark, he had no worries with Smooth, and the money he'd owed will soon be paid in full. Knock! knock! knock! Bo$$ woke up out of his nod. startled by Keto's knocking on the window. "Open the fucking door nigga!" Keto said while grabbing on the passenger's door handle. Hitting the power locks, Bo$$ unlocked the door for Keto. "What it do Keto?" He asked. "That bill you got in your hand. Let me hit that shit nigga!" Keto replied. "This ain't your lane right here! This that dog food nigga!" Bo$$ stated. "You keep that shit for yourself! I'm good! Let's get the fuck up outta here. Nicco's waiting on us." Keto stated. "Yo that money better be right. I ain't trying to hear no bullshit about nothing." Bo$$ said. "Everything's cool. The nigga knows what time it is!" Keto replied. "Good because if he don't, his ass gone learn tonight!" Bo$$ said. "Where's your man at who you doing the job with?" Keto asked. Nodding out behind the wheel and swerving Bo$$ paid no mind to Keto's question. "Bo$$!!" Keto yelled out. "What the fuck you doing?" He then asked. "You all swerving and shit like you can't function. If you crash. I'm out! I'm leaving your ass right where you at." Keto said in a scolding tone of voice. Laughing at what Keto said Bo$$ replied, "Shut your scared ass up! I know what's going on. I got the wheel nigga! We good!" "Make this right on Bidwell Ave and park right in front of that Z." Keto said.as he got out of the MPV, and walked up to Nicco's car, then got inside. "What's good Keto?" Nicco asked. "Same old shit, just a different day but in this case a different night." Keto stated. "I got my lil hitter in the MPV. Straight shooter. I told him about the job, and that you was gonna fill him in with all the details." Keto stated. "That's your responsibility! What I'm paying you for, if you can't handle the job?" Nicco asked. "You right!" Keto said. "I know damn well I am!" Nicco snapped back. "The bitch drives a purple 550SL coupe. You should already know what she looks like. Pretty as fuck, long wavy jet black hair. I mean the bitch hair is pass her ass long!" Nicco explained. "I know what she looks like. I'll be sure to point her out precisely!" Keto replied. "I need this shit done a.s.a.p." Nicco stated. "I can't have no delays with this job. The same way you and your hitter is getting paid up front, I expect to see the results of the compensation!" Nicco explained. "Take that backpack on the floor. Everything is there! 50 racks and the whole chicken! Get at me soon as you get off work!" Nicco stated. "I got you! You know what time it is!" Keto replied. Reaching into the backpack he took out two paper banded stacks of blue faces, and put them inside his jeans pocket before exiting the Z. Keto got back inside the MPV, as Bo$$ noticed a bulge inside his left jean pocket. Paying closer attention, he saw that it was money. How much money was the question Bo$$ asked himself. Sparking a conversation Bo$$ asked, "So what the nigga talking about? He paying or he playing?" "We good Bo$$. Everything right here! Your money, and a whole chicken that he wants me to slang for him." Keto stated. "You got the whole 30rackz and a kilo?" Bo$$ asked greedily! "Of course. I told you that shit was real." Keto replied. Thinking to himself if this nigga got thirty thousand in cash, plus a whole kilo he had to have a couple of bands in his pocket. Feeling played he was about to reverse the whole play! Bo$$ was about his business and didn't tolerate the snake shit. Continuing to think to himself. *"This nigga thinks just because I sniff a lil dope he can play me! The whole time this nigga really got paid for this job, but think he gone give me anything less than half! Shame on you!!"* "Bo$$ let's hit a side block or something so I can see what this cocaine is talking about!" Keto said. "Nigga fuck a side block we gone hit the park, and chill right where the playground at. It's after midnight so we good!" Bo$$ replied. Bo$$ pulled up and parked in a handicap space where it was dark. Perfect place to sit back and get fucked up! Keto gave Bo$$ his 30racks then took out the chicken and instantly tore into the plastic. Smelling the stench of the cocaine made Keto fart with excitement! His stomach started rumbling as he put a chunk of cocaine as big as a golf ball onto the back of an old scratch off. "Bust that down!" Keto said to Bo$$. Taking the bill back out of his pocket he put half of the coke on it and began crushing it up. Bo$$ was 'bout to speed ball knowing that he still had a nice amount of dope inside the bill. "Snifftt. snifft. sniffttt. snuftt!! Woooooohh!! This some good ass coke!" Bo$$ stated taking his first hit! Sniffftttt.sniffttt.snifffttttt.uhhh! Keto said then farted again. This time it sounded like he shitted on himself! High like the clouds he never seen it coming. "Bang! Bang!" As pieces of brain splattered the passenger's side window and door of the MPV. Reaching into Keto's pocket Bo$$ removed the money, as his body sat slouch in the passenger's seat. "Stupid ass nigga!" He called Keto before pushing his body out of the passenger's seat, onto the ground. Taking his shirt he immediately wiped the window off clean as possible, then the door, and tossed the shirt inside the backpack with the kilo. Starting the MPV, Bo$$ put it in drive and drove through the backside of Lincoln Park faster than the speed of light. Exiting on Communipaw Ave and keeping straight until he reached the light at Communipaw Ave and Rt.440. He ran the red light, paranoid and high, taking the Kearny bridge on his way back to Brick City. Things were looking bright for Bo$$. This was the easiest job yet he thought to himself. And all he did was kill the nigga that tried to play him like he was stupid. Talking out loud to himself, "All you had to do was play fair. I never would've tried to play you I never would've had to kill you! Don't nothing beat the cross, but the double cross." Looking in his rearview, Bo$$ felt a sense of relief, knowing that it was no traffic behind him. Back in Brick City, no traffic was out on the streetz this late in the hood unless it was 12 patrolling, or the Narcs hopping out on some shit! Making his way towards Hawthorne, Bo$$ decided to go check out a lil freak bitch who lived in that area. He needed to lay low for the rest of the night, and this would be the best place for him right now, until he can get situated and take care of things back in his own hood.

Driving through Hoboken, Nicco was making moves. All he thought about is how he was gonna make his claim to fame. Everything from slanging a hundred brickz and stacking paper, to buying something luxury, and finding a real connect so he can keeping his flow going. With 100k waiting on him in exchange for 3 brickz, nobody could tell him shit! He thought about bringing Shark to the table and letting him know what time it was with him hitting a niggaz safe. But at the same time he was like fuck Shark! "I'm that nigga now!" He said feeling himself like he'd been getting it out the mud for real. Turning up into IHOP parking lot Nicco saw the Red Acura RDX parked right in front of the window where Puerto Rican Papito sat. Focusing on the nigga truck Nicco said to himself, " I have to get me something luxury! This RDX is tight. All red with the black feet and matching red brake discs. I'm 'bout to step my shit up!" Looking through the window, Papito made a hand gesture, and a slim red bone got out of the passenger's side of the Acura and got into the Z with Nicco. "Who you?" Nicco asked lustfully. "You got that work or not?" The slim red bone chick asked. "Yea! You know I stays with the work!" He replied arrogantly. Taking the money out of her jacket she gave Nicco four thick knots then said. "A hundred bands!" Quickly he exchanged his end of the deal, watching as she tucked the 3 brickz inside her jacket. Before getting out of his car, she stated "At this price if it's good. We'll do further business." Then got out of the Z, and got back inside the Acura, as Papito came out and got in the driver's seat and pulled off. "That bitch was sexy, whoever the fuck she was. I would've gave her slim red ass a stack, with no problem for that pussy!" Nicco said out loud to himself. Thinking about the play he just made he knew that it would be more business to be dealt, as long as he had the coke to deal. Besides with his prices, all of Kiem's clientele was on its way out the window. With a couple more stops to make, Nicco wasn't planning on getting no sleep anytime soon unless he stumbled upon a bitch he could lay up with for the night. And with the money he put on Bliss's head he surely didn't want to be around when that action took place. Just thinking 'bout how crazy the streetz was ready to get he decided to hit South Jersey for a day or two. After all he only had a couple days, until his party at "Main Event."

    Killing the interstate all you could hear was the gears shift and the sound of the loud pipe as Kiem murdered the Ninja doing about 90mph. On the turnpike, coming up on their exit, Kiem switched gears and broke the bike down making a turn with ease before getting into his left lane, then making another left turn onto Garfield Ave. Riding a few blocks Kiem surveyed the area for 12, or any opp for that reason. Circling the blocked of their designated target, Kiem rode to the next block over, and backed the bike up to the curb allowing Bandz to get off. Turning the engine off and letting the kick stand down, Kiem then got off the bike and quickly stretched his legs, before making their move. Strapping both helmets onto the bikes seat, they both put on their ski mask and moved proficient. Creeping on the side of someone's house they made their way into the backyard, as Bandz quickly hopped the backyard gate with Kiem following. Hopping the next gate, they were both now in their target's backyard. Bandz reached in her backpack and took out a lock pick, then inserted the needle nose tip into the door lock and squeezed the trigger like handle until the lock completely bust open. Without a sound being made Bandz opened the door as they both entered the house in the pursuit of happiness. Moving through the living room, they took notice that no one was downstairs or in the kitchen. Creeping upstairs, they both laid eyes on Joany who was sitting at her bedroom table with her stem in her mouth smoking something heavy. Walking through her bedroom door, she paid no attention that two individuals stood before her dressed in all black with ski masks on. Joany was so high that when she looked up and did pay attention. Her first words were "Y'all better get the fuck up outta here before I call the damn police! Standing in my goddamn room looking like some assholes, dressed in black with your faces all covered up! Then you standing in my damn light and you see I'm tryna smoke! Mutha fuckas. Y'all just gone stand there huh? I…" as Bandz sucker punched the shit out her knocking the words right out her fucking mouth. Lifting her back up on her feet. "Bitcchhh!" Bandz called her as she hit her with a mean left hook to the jaw! "Where's Nicco?" Kiem asked. "Oh no! Don't tell me he done ran off with all your drugs". "I seen he had so much cocaine in his room, I just knew something wasn't right!" Joany replied. "Do you know who Unique was?" Bandz asked harshly. "Unique?" Joany asked. "BITCH. I'm not even gone play with you! Unique was my mother. Ya bastard ass son's father Nicholas, is who killed my mother." Bandz said coldly as ever. "You're familiar with Karma Estelvo right?" Bandz asked. "Wait, let me explain. I can explain everything." Joany replied. Smmaaccckkk!!! Bandz pistol whipped her across the jaw. Blood seeped from the corners of her mouth, as her jaw hung dislocated. Trying to mumble Kiem dragged her ass back to the chair she was sitting in when they entered the room. Bandz took out a roll of duct tape, and bound both her ankles to the chair legs then did both her wrists the same. With Joany not being able to put up any kind of struggle Bandz removed a 12" razor wire from her backpack, then a pair of wire proof gloves. Lighting up cigarette after cigarette she began to put each one of them out, all over Joany's face and neck, burning her to the white meat! With only two cigarettes left Bandz lit both, and put each one of 'em out in Joany's eyes, burning her eyes to the sockets! "Muuummmhhh!" was the mummy like sounds that Joany made from the excruciating pain. Kiem felt everything that Bandz was feeling at that very moment run through his veins. Putting on her wire proof gloves Bandz grabbed the razor wire and wrapped it around Joany's neck so tight that the razor wire ripped her neck open instantly, squirting blood everywhere. Pulling the wire tight as she could she wrapped it around her neck a second time, as the razors tore into her jugular veins making her cough up thick spurts of blood! Finishing the job Bandz wrapped the razor wire around her face and head, cutting her face open the way that a coroner cuts open a dead person's chest cavity to remove its organs. Then she said "this is for my mother" and snapped Joany's neck! The sound was gruesome, and Kiem knew that Bandz was with the shitz but not with the bullshit like this! He thought that Bliss was ill with it, but by far Bandz had her beat! "Come on Ma! Let's dip" Kiem said. "Hold up my G! Got one last thing to handle." Bandz replied. Taking her backpack off, she unzipped the main compartment and removed a red biohazard bag. Running to the second bedroom which was Nicco's room she turned on the lights and walked over to his bed then opened the biohazard bag and dumped a rat on his pillow with its throat cut open. "What the fuuccckkkk!!!" Kiem said in disbelief. "Yea! You know his popz was a rat, which means he was raisin' mice! Like father, like son! Let's get ghost nigga!" Bandz commanded. Racing back downstairs through the backdoor and hitting the backyard they quickly hopped the first gate, then the second, and crept low key back past the side of the same house. Reaching the front, they snatched up their helmets and put 'em on, as Bandz got on the bike first and told Kiem to get on.

Following her command, Kiem grabbed her by the waistline as she started the bike and gassed the throttle crazily. Hitting the clutch they instantly took off making a run for the interstate. Coming up on a red light Bandz played with the break constantly hitting it making the tail end of the bike jump while looking back at Kiem! Suddenly the light turned green, and Bandz literally showed her ass. She hit the clutch and switched gears as the Ninja swept into the darkness!

Shoving all the money into his pockets Bo$$ snatched up the backpack and jumped out the MPV. Walking towards the apartment building where his lil freak bitch stayed, he entered the building and hurried upstairs. Banging on the door, a light voice came from the other side sounding annoyed, "Whooo is it?" "It's me. Open the door! Hurry up!!" Bo$$ nervously replied. Hearing the locks click, the door opened as Bo$$ entered quickly and locked the door back. Trying not to raise no suspicions, he complimented the shorty. "I have to be honest with you shorty! You look real seductive with ya t-shirt and panties on! If I ain't know no better I couldn't tell you, or Adina Howard apart." "Umm hmm!" She replied but smiling at the same time. Bo$$ knew that she was buying the bullshit! "Come here!" He stated as he palmed her backside. Turning around into his arms, she hugged him passionately in hopes that he might have some get high. "Why you always come through so late?" She asked. "I be on the block all day shorty. I can't make no money if I'm up under you all day!" He replied. "So all you come here for is just to get high and fuck?" She asked sounding annoyed. "That's not just it. You forgot about me getting my dick sucked, and that good ass meatloaf you make." He replied laughing. "Get the hell off me! Your ass makes me sick!" She stated. "Look. You know you my shorty, I was just fucking with you! Stop being all sensitive and keep doing your part! Long as I do what I'm supposed to do, you should have no complaints! Now get your thick ass over here and help me count this money!" He said seriously. Taking the money out his pocket that he took from Keto, he stuffed it down her panties, and told her to make sure the count is right! "I gotta use the bathroom right quick. Get that count right! If it's all there, I'm gonna do something nice for you!" He stated not knowing how much was there, but he had to make it sound good. Removing both guns from his waist, he put the 9mm on the bedroom nightstand, and took the 38special into the bathroom with him! Removing the remaining four bullets first, he then removed the two empty shell casings, wiped them off, then wrapped 'em in toilet tissue, and flushed them. After reloading the gun, he quickly tucked it into the backpack, then took the rest of the money out of his pockets! Looking at the money still in its original bands, he felt no need to count it. Wondering how much money shorty was counting, he decided to take a quick shower. Grabbing the bottle of ammonia, he drenched down with it then scrubbed continuously with some soap. After 10 minutes in the water, he got out looking for a towel. With nothing in sight for him to dry off with he did some real ghetto shit! Used the bathroom floor mat then put it back in its original spot. Stepping back into the bedroom, shorty was on the bed ass naked with her legs spread apart, with all the money displayed right where her love box would be visible. "I counted it twice. It's twenty thousand!" She stated. "Who you rob?" She nosily asked. "What the fuck I tell you about questioning my money?" Bo$$ snapped at her! "You winning right now, this ya last time. Side bitches gone be winning next!" He said angrily. Taking the folded bill out of his small pants pocket, he opened it up and took a two on two! Snift. Sniffttt! Sniff. Sniffttt! "Let me get some." She anxiously requested. Thinking about the money he paid her no mind! "Fifty thousand and a whole kilo! I can't believe that nigga! One thing about it. When you do dirt, you get dirt! He thought to himself. Taking another 2on2. Sniffttt, Sniffttt! Sniffttt. Sniffttt! Instantly he drifted off feeling the effects of the coke and dope mix. Deep in his nod he never felt shorty go down on him. Spitting and slobbering all over his tool, she bit down on the head as he briefly woke up out of his nod! Polishing the dick like some expensive marble she managed to ask. "You not gonna give me none?" Feeling the sensation of her deep throat which got him fully erect, he reached for the backpack and took out the brick. Still sucking, nibbling, slobbering, and deep throating she acted like she didn't notice him pull out all that coke. Tearing back into the plastic he broke off a grape size piece of cocaine. "Here!" he said as he handed her the coke. Looking like a puppy with excitement in its eyes, she greedily broke a piece off, and began crushing it up on a bill. Dumping the coke out of the bill and onto a medium size cosmetic mirror she then went to work! Sniff! Sniff! Sniff! Ooohh!! "This coke is the best shit that I've ever had! Where you get this from?" She excitedly asked. "You need to get your hands on plenty more of this! We can make some real money and never look back!" She stated. Liking the sound of what he just heard he knew that he had enough coke to make a profit, but trying to re up on this same quality would be the only problem. "We gonna make some real money. All you have to do is keep ya fucking mouth closed. Can't have niggaz blazing at me trying to take my place. Know what I mean!" Bo$$ stated. "Also, get me up when all the stores start opening! Gotta do a lil shopping." He bragged. "I know that's right. I'm going shopping too!" She stated then got on all fours and said to Bo$$ "Now come fuck me like I stole something!" "Fuck me like this pussy is going out of style!" She demanded. Getting right up behind her he inserted himself, then grabbed her by the waist and began stroking her long and deep! "Ohhh! Oohhh! Fuck me baby. Fuck me baby! I love this dope dick. I love it! Nod off in this pussy daddy! Fuck me. Yesss! Fuck me right there! Fuck me you bastard! Fuck me!" She yelled out. "I'm fucking you! I. Am. Fucking. You!" He replied with every stroke. "I can't feel my fucking legs. I'm numb! I'm numb!" He stated. "I don't care you better fuck me!! Put that dick up in my stomach! Oohhh!! Just like that. Just. Like. That!" She replied. And within a few moments, Bo$$ reached up and slightly choked her, while he released himself deep inside her! Panting like a wounded deer, fighting for life they both laid there trying to recuperate, but fell asleep!

Riding around with 167k on him, all profit from moving five brickz made Nicco feel like a superstar! He never had this much money in his possession that belonged solely to him. And at a flat rate of $33.5k, he knew that more money was sure to come. Passing a few car lots as he approached the boardwalk, made his head turn at almost everything he drove past. Sitting graciously on a display ramp, sat an all Red Challenger SRT HellCat Red Eye. Immediately pulling over, he got out of his car to further examine the HellCat. Talking out loud to himself. "All Red with Black 24"rims and all Black leather interior. "I want this bitch here!" Looking at the price tag on the windshield made

moving at a steady pace striving not to give too much attention to the crime scene. "Whatever happened it'll be on the twelve o'clock news!" Nice said to himself.

In route to Atlantic City Karma was feeling the urge to explode. She dreamt of the moment when she would be able to enjoy the view of adult play, up close and personal., then enjoy herself in more ways than one! She knew that Mr. Pairings was the factor to rehabilitate her multi-million-dollar enterprise, after its collapse from dissatisfied employees. Just thinking about his masculine manifestation made her nipples erect and her cat super moist. Clawing the leather seats of the Continental while being driven to her destination, Karma fixed her mind on one thing, and that was getting whoever and whatever out of the way that stopped her from being victorious. Arriving at the Marriott she was excited because she needed a relief! Making her way up to room 551, the elevator stopped as she stepped off and walked a couple feet before standing directly in front of Nicco's room. As she knocked on the door, she could hear footsteps on the other side creeping up to the door. As the door swung open, Karma walked in, noticing that Nicco was edgy. "Karma like I've already explained. Everything is in motion for that bitch to be gone out of your way! Whatever she done is none of my business, but this isn't something I'd suggest rushing. However, I can assure you that I will exceed on our agreement and execute this situation by the weekend." Nicco expressed. "Everything is going to take its course. I've been running around hustling nonstop getting ya portion of the money up to show you that I can handle things." Reaching inside of his jacket pocket, he removed four thick stacks of money and handed it to Karma. "It's 100k like I told you. You can count it!" "There's no need to count behind you darling! This is not preschool. Unless you want to become dinner for the sharks, I know very damn well that you will execute upon our agreement!" Karma rudely stated. "Furthermore, I do applaud your hustle." She said as she clapped in a sarcastic manner. "Now tell me, what is it that you seek my help with?" Karma asked while staring Nicco dead in his eyes. Looking down at the floor, Nicco explained. "I remember you telling me that I need to advance my game, and how I needed to get a car 'cuz I only had a ride! But the problem is, I don't have a license or insurance, but I have the money up now to buy something nice. I was just hoping that you could somehow help me out." "Are you serious darling?" Karma asked sarcastically. Not feeling her response, Nicco used reverse psychology on her and hoped that it would work to his advantage. "Look. I've never asked you for shit really! You're the one that called me with this get rich scheme, 'bout how you know where it's plenty of money and drugs at. And all I had to do was just go in, empty the safe, and give you a percentage of the profit. Then you come to me with some shit, 'bout killing some bitch. For what, I don't know. And you can't help me get the car that I want?! If I go to jail behind doing this shit you think the streetz gone give a fuck, if I'm a rat?" Nicco asked boldly as ever. Karma looked at him in silence. Nicco continued. "Just like I fucking thought, nothing to say huh?!" "Darling. I didn't mean to offend you, but you're wiser that what I thought!" Karma stated. "If having something luxury is what you desire, I suppose we can arrange that. Only on one condition." Karma said. "Here we go with this shit again!" Nicco replied. "What's the condition?" "I want you to eat my pussy! The same way you desire luxury, I desire an orgasm!" Karma expressed as she leaned back on the bed and lifted her skirt.

     Knocked out cold and snoring like a wild boar, she removed Bo$$ arm from around her. She crept out of the bed and lurked towards the backpack. Opening its zipper, she reached inside and quietly pulled out, what she thought was the cocaine. Startled by the bloody T- shirt, with a bunch of slimy looking dried up snot all over it. She reached back inside and removed the kilo. Not knowing how much cocaine it exactly was her eyes grew big in size as her stomach started twisting in knots. Excited from having her hands on so much coke, she quickly tore into the plastic and removed a few big chunks! Fixing the plastic back, making it look as if no one touched it, she put the kilo back inside the backpack along with the T-shirt, and zipped it closed. Taking her stash and hiding it inside of an empty rice box, she placed the box inside the refrigerator then went and woke Bo$$ up! "Bo$$. Bo$$! Get up!" She yelled. "Mann! What time is it shorty?" Bo$$ asked. "If you don't get ya ass up! Most of the stores are open now. It's almost noon!" She replied. "Aight. Aight. I'm up!" He replied as he wiped the cold from his eyes. "Look. I'm gone drop you off downtown, so you can do a little shopping. I have to go catch up on some shit in my hood! After that I'll get back up with you, and we can just chill and do us!" Bo$$ stated. "What the fuck ever Bo$$!" She replied in an upset tone. "Shorty you really getting on my fucking nerves right now! I told you that we'll get back up later, and you still on some tryna cuff a nigga type shit! Right now ain't the time to be boo'd up. I got shit to take care of. What part of that you don't understand. It's like the more I teach you, the dumber you get!" He said sounding irritated. "Fuck you, mutha fucka! You the only dumb bitch around here!" She snapped back. Heading to the bathroom, Bo$$ could hear the water running, as he reached for his jeans. Making sure that she didn't hit his pockets, he removed the money that was still in the bands smiled, and quickly shoved it back inside his pockets. Now up with his clothes on, and ready to get things moving, Shorty came out of the bathroom, and threw on some sweatpants, a pair of Timbs, and a T-shirt. "Let me get a wake up! I'm already on some stupid shit so I ain't tryna hear nothing!" She said to Bo$$. "What the fuck you gotta attitude for?" He asked harshly. Not saying shit in return she just stood there and held her hand out. "This shit getting old!" He stated while reaching into his backpack. Pulling out the coke, he just broke a piece off, and slammed it into her hand. "Here you go bitch! Enjoy!" He coldly stated. "You think I ain't!" She replied sarcastically. Shaking his head, he snatched up the money that was already counted, and peeled off twenty blue faces. "This should be enough for you to get a few nice fits." He said while handing her the money. "What about my hair and shit?" She complained. "Fuck ya hair! You better throw a wig or some shit on!" He fired back. "Yous a sorry ass nigga you know that!" "If I'm that sorry, what that make you? Always fiending. You one step away from having a glass dick in ya mouth!" He harshly stated. "Oh! You really gonna go there huh?" She shamefully asked. "That's aight. Shine nigga! Cuz my time coming!" She said confidently. "Can we just get the fuck up outta here? I really gotta get moving." Bo$$ stated. "Here. Take this extra five hundred and get ya hair and shit done!" Grabbing the money out of his hand quickly, she kissed him on the cheek, then thanked him. Bo$$ quickly stuffed the rest of the money into his pockets, then grabbed his 9mm of the nightstand.

On their way out the door he felt untouchable. He now had money to blow as the blow (cocaine) and would soon be back on the block, getting more money. Only difference now is that he can pay off his debt and run a few packs up! And he wouldn't have to lie 'bout the money being short, or the dope coming up missing, ' cuz he could pay for it upfront. He thought to himself this was the break that he needed, so he had to stay afloat no matter what. "No matter what!" He said out loud then started they MPV. "What you talking to ya self now?" She asked giggling. "Ain't shit funny shorty! Just thinking that's all."

Brushing his teeth for the second time, he couldn't believe that he just ate some old foreign bitch out. But for the love of that HellCat he'll surely do it again. Calling Keto's phone to check on that situation, his phone just rang out, and went to voicemail. Talking out loud to himself, Nicco started to curse the nigga out. "Why the fuck you not picking up! I know you better had took care of shit! The last thing you want. Is to have me on ya ass! You better off fucking with the police, instead of fucking with a real nigga!"

Hearing a phone ring Bo$$ knew that it wasn't his phone, and his freak bitch ain't own a phone! The phone continuously rang, as she reached underneath the passenger's seat, and pulled out the LG. Looking suspect Bo$$ thought to himself that it had to be Keto's phone! The nigga must have dropped his fucking phone. "Who phone is this?" She asked. "You got another phone for some thot bitches?!" She said angrily. "Shorty. I ain't got another phone for no bitches! My nigga must have dropped his shit when he was getting out last night." "Well ain't you gonna call him back and let him know you got it?" She asked. "I'll just take it to him once I get out the hood. It's no big deal!" Bo$$ replied trying to stop her from asking questions. He decided to stroke her ego. "I know ya hair and nails better be tight when I come scoop you later. And I wanna see you in something tight like a glove! Ain't no need to have all that ass if you not gone flaunt it!" Bo$$ explained. The blushing and biting on her lips let Bo$$ know that she was feeling good about his compliments towards her! Parking in front of Dr Jay's, they both got out and went inside. Snatching up a few pair of jeans, a couple shirts, and some Timbs. Bo$$ was ready to hit the check out counter and bounce! "Look shorty, I'm 'bout to go take care of some things, you got more than enough money to do you, and get back to the crib. Just make sure everything is everything, once I'm on my way!" Bo$$ stated. "You know that I always do, so you ain't got to remind me." She replied.

Watching a repeat of The View. Nice turned the volume up on the TV and paid close attention to the Breaking News Report! "Good afternoon! I'm Sara Buck. and I'm Ted Nero. and we bring you this Breaking News Report! Where the body of an unidentified man was found earlier this morning in Lincoln Park, who suffered two gunshot wounds to the head. Right now police have no leads, nor possible suspects and they are asking anyone with information to please call 1-800 Crime Stoppers! Remember you can remain anonymous and receive a cash reward for up to $5,000." "Damn I wonder who the fuck that was!" Nice stated while calling Kiem. Hearing his phone vibrate drove him crazy, especially being that he just not so long ago got in the house, turning over to reach for his phone, he saw that it was Nice calling and instantly answered. "Yo! What's good?" Kiem asked. "Bro! You see the news?" Nice asked. "Nah. I just woke up. What's going on though?" Kiem asked. "Some nigga got dome checked in Lincoln Park. Whoever did it, hit him twice. Twelve don't have no leads or nothing." Nice replied. "Turn to Fox. It's breaking news right now!" Nice stated. "Nigga I'm not even in the city right now! The show is on the road, but I'll be back within a few days. I'll check out the news feed on my phone when I get up!" Kiem stated. "Already!" Nice replied. "I'll holla at you then my nigga! 1lif!" Kiem replied then hung up. Not too pressed about who just got clipped, Kiem didn't give it too much thought tryna figure out who the nigga was. Whoever he was, somebody just cleaned his clock!

Feeling a bit relieved but knowing no orgasm could conquer the rage that was building inside of her. Frustrated from the disappointment of being ignored, she knew the risk that would develop from her own lost connections and skeletons in her closet! Still Karma was an extremist who promised many hope. Arriving at the warehouse in Cherry Hill, she was anxious to inventory the new arrivals. Strutting with a briefcase in her hand, she made her way deep into the warehouse, where she was greeted by a younger, tall, redheaded woman. They both kissed one another upon their cheeks, as they spoke in Russian. Two men who stood holding M-16's, guarding the door to a room that was labeled the vault instantly stepped aside allowing Karma and the other woman access. Smiling from ear to ear, Karma was thrilled by the three young girls from Malaysia, that were ravishing. The three girls from Sabah were pygmy but indeed beautiful. And the four teenage girls from Sri Lanka were enough for any savage to feast. But the two young girls from the Philippines were time pieces. Karma knew that this dozen was an immaculate choice. Very pleased with the selection, she spoke in Russian to the other woman, then handed her the briefcase. Two Million Dollars was the price tag. Knowing that customers would twirl for this ultimate young blood thrilled by the thought of these young girls' maximum performance. Karma knew what mattered most called for desperate measures. Speaking in Russian once again, Karma then shook hands with the redheaded woman, before parting ways.

Sitting in his car parked in front of the corner store building, Shark waited for Cheebah to come downstairs, so they could make a few runs. Not paying attention to the Red HellCat that was parked directly across the street from her apartment building, Cheebah came downstairs and glanced at the car, imagining how she'd look behind the wheel. Getting into the Beamer with Shark, she couldn't help herself but to look across the street at the car once again while not paying attention to Shark when he asked her how she was doing. In his feelings 'cuz she ignored him, he questioned her like she was his everyday companion. "What you got some shit on ya mind or something you wanna tell me about?" Shark asked. Rolling her eyes at him in disgust she replied. "Look not right now! I'm not even beat for the bullshit with you." "Bitch! I can't tell. I asked you how you were doing, and you straight ignored me. But broke ya damn neck to look across the street." He angrily replied. "Nigga. I'm not even gonna pay ya ass no mind! You act like we in a committed relationship." Cheebah stated. "No problem. remember that shit when ya lights get turned off!" Shark replied. "Hold up! You ain't the only nigga out here with money." She rubbed in his face. "And you ain't the only bitch out here with a pussy!" He shot back. "You right! But the average bitch ain't gone do what I do." Cheebah said. "Ya right! The average bitch ain't gone do what you do. But a freak bitch gone do it all for a dollar! Ain't that how we started fucking around!" Shark replied sarcastically. "Nicco ain't think I was a freak bitch when he was diving all in this pussy! Ask him. That nigga fucks me well!" Cheebah said seriously. "Bitch! Get the fuck out my car! Get ya thot ass out now! Get Nicco to take care of ya utilities and shit!" Shark screamed on her. "Oh what you think he ain't?!" She replied sarcastically. She slammed the hell out of his car door breaking the passenger's side window as she got out. "And I've been fucking him the whole time we been seeing each other!" She said. Nothing else was said as the BMW back tires burned rubber, leaving clouds of smoke while pulling off. Feeling like a sucker now. Shark's only thought, was to beat the fuck out of Nicco. Talking out loud to himself. "Imma fuck this nigga up! I ain't even gone say shit right now, Imma catch his ass at his own party!" Thinking back on plenty of times when he could have tricked with Nicco's mom for some crack. "I should've let ya moms suck my dick and hit her from the back but that's what I get for playing fair with ya bitch ass! Not anymore!"

Back out in the Weequahic section, Bo$$ stood posted up on the block, chopping it up with a couple of niggaz, while blowing on a swisher. Fresh to death he felt good being back in the hood, knowing that he now had a hell of a advantage over everybody else that he hustled with. Waiting for Smooth to come through so he could try to fix what he fucked up, he started to get lightheaded and feel sick to his stomach, knowing that he needed a fix. Digging into his pocket for the candy bar, hoping that something sweet will hold him over, only made shit worst, as he bit into the Whatchamacallit. Now hunched over and ready to vomit, he suddenly felt relieved as he seen the chrome grill on the Dark Brown Wraith pull up. Rolling down his passenger's side window, Smooth called one of the young niggaz over and handed him a Timberland box. Bo$$ already knew that was the dope drop off and exactly how much. With no expression on his face Smooth caught eye contact with Bo$$ and nodded his head toward the passenger side door. "Get in!" Smooth directed in a calm but stern voice. Not knowing what the nigga intentions were, Bo$$ was kinda hesitant to get in. Even though he had all the money that he fucked up, he still thought twice. "Nigga. I ain't got all day!" Smooth said to Bo$$, causing him to pick up the pace and take his position in the passenger seat. Without looking in Bo$$ direction, Smooth adjusted in his seat while putting his car back into drive and said calm but firmly, "What I tell you 'bout being out here, if you ain't have that money? Didn't I tell you, I don't wanna see you out the here 'til all debts get paid!" he slightly paused and looked Bo$$ in the eyes before continuing "That means you can't be out here, eat out here, or even walk through here until I get my money!" Smooth stated harshly. Feeling the pressure but confident about having something rather than nothing to give to Smooth he smiled and stated "Smooth. Pipe down big homie! I told you I got you, once my lil shorty got her financial aid from ECC (Essex County College)." Reaching into his pocket, he pulled out the $3,000 that he fucked up. "Here!" Then gave Smooth the money. "Okay! I see you tryna get right!" Smooth stated as he took the money. "Tell you what! You can get back out here and eat, but you can't be out here fucking my money up! It's small change compared to my net worth, but at the end of the day, it's all about the count! And that count need to be correct!" Smooth expressed. Opening the center console, Smooth removed a brown paper bag, then handed it to Bo$$. "It's 35 bundles. Bring me back $2,100! The rest is you." Smooth stated. "I got you Smooth! Shit is gonna be straight from here on out!" Bo$$ said. "But I fucks with ya whip! This shit is big like a spaceship inside. I ain't never been inside nothing this luxurious in my life." Bo$$ stated. "This shit is nothing. You can have the same shit, even better! All you have to do is get ya mind right and focus! The money is out here. It's all on you and what you do with your opportunities, bullshit or get that bag!" Smooth stated. "You know Imma get that bag!" Bo$$ replied. "Imma get with you!" Smooth stated as Bo$$ got out the car. Standing there looking at the expensive machine accelerate Bo$$ had his mind made up, that he was getting to that bag no matter what! Even if he had to dead shit!

Reading the text that Kiem sent, Bliss couldn't stop smiling even if she wanted to! This was by far, the best wake up moment she ever experienced besides waking up next to him! Feeling a little poetic, she sent a text back, "It is such a blessing to have someone like you! You simply can't imagine how much you've helped me to become the woman that I am today. To know that I have someone who will listen with concern and help me through each trial is beyond measure. My loyalty is to you forevermore! XoXo Bliss." Buzz. Buzz. Buzz. Buzz. Buzz. Buzz! Mad as fuck, 'cuz his phone kept vibrating waking him up out of his rest, he reached for the Galaxy only to discover that it was now his connect calling him. "Talk to me!" Kiem stated as he answered the phone. "Okay! I'm on my way." Kiem replied. Now fully awake. he got up out of the bed and started getting himself together. Smelling the potency of the RPK he knew that Don Smoke was awake as well, if not Bandz too! Fully dressed in a cream-colored Massimo Alba two-piece suit with navy blue pinstripes, Kiem put on his suede navy blue loafers to set the outfit off. Heading downstairs the weed smell got stronger as he entered the den and found both Don Smoke and Bandz blowing heavy! "Oooh! Look at u!" Bandz stated. "Where you goin dressed all fly?" She asked. "I gotta make an important run right now!" Kiem replied. "Bro! I'm gone need you and Bandz to make a few rounds out here in New Castle, then hit Wilmington. Then we'll all link up in Dover. I gotta run out to DC right quick! But I'll be back soon as I can." Kiem stated. "Yo! You still got some Molly on deck?" Kiem asked. "Nigga! You know I stay with it." Don Smoke replied. "Kool 'cuz I need like a pool shot (2.5 grams) I gotta stay up. Ain't had a chance to get no rest for real!" "Say less my nigga! Look in the kitchen drawer, it's all you!" Don Smoke replied. "Good look!" Kiem stated then saluted Don Smoke.

Kiem grabbed the Molly and chased it down with some water, while simultaneously concealing his gun in his waistband. Noticing that the black trash bag wasn't by the garage door anymore he knew that Don Smoke had set the bag out for garbage pickup. Kiem hopped in his car in route towards his destination. He was confused as to what the urgency was that caused his connect to need to see him immediately! He couldn't make sense of anything so he just traveled the journey.

Please, accept it!" Then handed her a manilla envelope. "Thank You Mr. Vyntura. I greatly appreciate your kindness!" She stated then placed the manilla envelope inside of her briefcase. "I need to get a move on things." Kym expressed. "I will be in touch with you Mr.Vyntura!" "Very well then!" Oscar replied. "And you. You should move sooner than possible!" She said to Kiem before getting up from the table and exiting the restaurant. "My friend! It is always a delight to know that you are well prepared for any situation that may occur!" Oscar stated. "I have something for you! You have to understand that you're no longer on a level where you have to elevate. Your character is defined. You give the orders and pull the strings! Your hands are to stay clean from all work that can be outsourced!" Oscar expressed. "Am I making things vivid for you, my friend?" Oscar asked. Processing everything that he just was told, Kiem nodded his head in agreement, while thinking 'bout what this meant for him and his squad. Looking at his connect, he thanked him while shaking his hand. Oscar stood to his feet and extended his arms. As Kiem rose to his feet, Oscar greeted him with a hug! This moment was like some real movie type shit, Kiem thought to himself, but it was all real! After the embrace, both men sat back at the table as Oscar reached into his blazer pocket and removed a ring box. Opening the box, it revealed a 24k Yellow Gold Men's ring with a 5 carat Bezel-Set Emerald Cut Center, surrounded by rows of Melee, being 5.50 carats. Kiem looked fascinated by its design but valued the meaning behind it. Oscar removed the ring from its box and dropped it inside of Kiem's glass! It was more than enough ice, to keep his shot of Uncle Nearest 1856 on chill. Raising their shot glasses in the air, they both made a toast then tossed their drink back. Kiem managed not to swallow the ring, as he spit it back out into the palm of his hand. Instantly his connect took his handkerchief and blotted the ring, before placing it one Kiem's left pinky finger. Taking the billfold out of his pocket, Oscar counted out five one hundred dollar bills, then placed them on the table. "Come my friend! I want to show you something!" Oscar stated. Exiting the restaurant, they walked a few feet from where Kiem's car was parked, and stood in front of an all silver Porsche Panamera. "You like?" Oscar asked. "Yea! It's fly!" Kiem replied. "Just your style, huh?" Oscar asked. "No doubt. It's definitely my style!" Kiem replied. Checking out the 24" chrome feet with the full panoramic roof top made the Porsche look impeccable. The light grey leather interior complemented the exterior very well. The all chrome grill matched the chrome window trim as well as the twin duals on the back of the Panamera. Thinking 'bout how he was gonna have to get the CT-6 towed back, his connect read his mind. "My friend! You no need this vehicle anymore! I will have my men transport and discard of it. You have to stay under the radar much as possible. Switching vehicles is like chameleon for you!" Oscar explained then gave Kiem the smart key. "Get inside my friend. I will show you something!" Oscar stated. As they both got inside the car, his connect told him to start the engine. Once the Porsche was running, his connect instructed him to touch the dash screen. Doing as he was instructed, Kiem touched the screen with his index finger. Instantly the backseat of the Panamera rotated, revealing a gold-plated AR Assault Rifle, with two hundred round drums! Smiling at his new toy, Kiem knew that his connect was making sure that he had all the necessary fire power to destroy shit if he had too! "It needs no lock code! It is designed to recognize your fingerprint, and it is quick and accessible for your convenience. Even when you have the engine turned off, you will still be able to access the stash box now that you have activated the print recognition. And it can also hold up to 500 kilos." His connect explained. "My friend! I have other business that needs to be attended to. We will gather again and discuss further business!" His connect stated. Shaking his hand, Kiem thanked him for everything and was grateful for the opportunity of being in the position. Still, he knew that he had to finish Nicco's ass without a shadow of a doubt! "Snitch mutha fucka!!" Kiem said under his breath as his connect got out of the car. Kiem's mind was already focused on how everything would take place. At that very moment he understood that he no longer had to get his hands dirty. However this was something that he needed to handle himself. And it didn't stop there, 'cuz Ms. Estelvo had a surprise coming too! It was a setup the whole time. But the reason is what troubled Kiem the most! Putting the Porsche in drive, he eased out of the parking lot turning back on N St. NW and headed for the highway.

Now in Wilmington Don Smoke and Bandz hit every street and projects that was on the agenda. The timing was perfect 'cuz everyone was waiting for the drop. It's been dry since Don Smoke had made the last run. The product was moving twice as fast, and the demand for weight was at an all-time high! Nobody around had better product than Kiem and his squad. Word got 'round quick 'bout how good the cocaine was. And with clientele like that the squad was 'bout to have the streetz on smash! Only difference now, the show would go on the road. State to state, city to city! Don Smoke and Kiem, both had out of state clientele. They both had their own photographers (shooters), and they both had niggaz that showed 'em love! All the niggaz that did hate, did it from a distance. But it came with the territory! Shit like that was to be expected when you winning. Anything less, you'd be a damn fool! Don Smoke was deep in thought when his phone automated voice sounded through the Bluetooth. "Kiem is calling." "Kiem! What's shaking my nigga?" Don Smoke asked as he answered the phone. "Business as usual!" Kiem replied. "Where y'all at?" "Bout 25 mins from Dover!" Don Smoke answered. "All the drops was straight?" Kiem asked. "You already know!" Don Smoke replied. "Yo! Hit Dover Downs. Meet me by the slot machines to the right of the entrance. We 'bout to have a lil fun time!" Kiem stated. "Say less bro! View you when you get there!" Don Smoke replied.

The night was approaching, and Nicco couldn't wait to get back! Not caring if Keto and his goon took care of business or not, all he was worrying 'bout was the HellCat! Speeding on the interstate, he was in route to Cheebah's apartment. Not worried if Shark would be there, 'cuz he knew that Cheebah would have texted him, this was the grimy type of shit that Nicco got a kick out of doing. Thinking about his next move after his party at Main Event, Nicco never felt such an urge of power in his life! I'll throw a couple of brickz out here in the streetz then I'll bounce down south! South Carolina or somewhere, where I can just chill. and do my thizzle! He thought to himself. Hitting Jersey city. Parking directly in front of Cheebah's apartment building he hurried out of the car, as Cheebah came downstairs to meet him. Holding the smart key in her hand she smiled at him mischievously, then kissed him on the lips. "Hey baby!" She greeted him while dangling the smart key between her thumb and index finger. Too anxious to get behind the wheel of his new whip, he paid her no mind! Taking the key out of her hand, he told her to get inside as he unlocked the doors. "You like my new shit?" He arrogantly asked. "Yeessss baby! This is all you right here! I love the way the new leather smells!" Cheebah replied. "This is what you call money! And niggaz think you ain't that nigga! Watch their face when you pull up baby!" She exaggerated gassing his head up! "I know right! Niggaz gonna be asking me for jobs!" Nicco said in a stern, but arrogant tone of voice. "Listen. You can hold the keys to the Z if you want! I got some things to take care of, so I know you can use the wheels to handle your priorities. We good with each other long as things stay between us!" He explained. Looking like she just seen death she thought about her conversation earlier with Shark, before saying. "Baby you know we good! Stop being bitch made worrying about the next nigga!" Not feeling her comment, he tossed her the keys to the Z, then reached into his pocket and gave her a few blue faces. "I gotta go check on some shit, it's late and I supposed to been at my destination! We'll get up this weekend after my party!" Nicco explained. "Ain't no thang! I'll catch you this weekend baby!" She replied then pecked him on the lips, before getting out of the car. Push starting the HellCat, the engine spoke power, as Nicco stepped on the accelerator. Thrilled by the roar of the engine, he couldn't wait to ride through the city! Even more than ever, he couldn't wait to pull up at Main Event! Putting the HellCat in drive. he pulled off crazily like he wanted to get stopped by the police. "Attention seeking ass nigga!" Cheebah said to herself while walking back into her building. Turning onto Garfield Ave., Nicco decided to take that way home to avoid any unnecessary attention. It was after midnight and he been up all day. The streetz looked normal and quiet and dark like always! Now wondering to himself if the job with Bliss was taken care of, he decided that he would hit Keto up in the morning to check on things. Pulling up in front of his house, he cut the engine off, and sat inside his car thinking. Ready for Main Event, he had less than 48 hours and he would take the streetz by surprise with his remarkable prices! Popping some Xanax Nicco felt the nod coming on. Pancakes and syrup was his thing, but lately it's been hard for him to get his hands on some official lean. Usually he'll pour about a four and be good for the whole day. But now that he had some paper, he was thinking more like four liters! Getting his hands on something like that would last him a few weeks easy! But getting it was the problem. Thinking about Bandz sexy ass, he hoped that she would attend his party, and bring her boss so that he could negotiate his prices with her. He knew that Gi-Gi was copping work from Kiem, and he knew Kiem's prices. But in order to take the streetz he had to beat the competition. If he was able to develop some kind of relationship with Bandz, he knew that they would surely take off! Fantasizing about Bandz he dozed off!

Pulling into Dover Downs parking lot, Kiem circled the lot halfway, in search of Don Smoke's car. Now making the full circle, he spotted the R8 parked between a Ford F-150 and a Chevy Avalanche which made it hard to locate. Gliding into an empty parking space right across from the R8, Kiem put the Panamera in park then removed his gun from in back of his waist and placed it underneath his driver's seat. Getting out of the car, a group of women looked Kiem up and down, like he was a full course dinner, while complimenting his car and his pinstripe suit. "Thank you Ladies! Thank you!" Kiem said to the women for their compliments. As he walked towards the casino entrance, the group of women walked in the same direction, and one of them asked, "Can I walk with you?" "Sure! Ain't no harm in us walking together." Kiem replied. "How are you? My name is Angela." "It's nice to meet you Ms. Angela, I'm Kiem! Just on my way to meet a few friends and enjoy the atmosphere!" Kiem stated. "I know that's right! It's my girl's birthday, so me and some friends decided to take her out for the night". Angela stated. "That was very thoughtful of you all." Kiem stated. Walking through the electric slide doors, Kiem seen Bandz over at the slot machines and knew Don Smoke was in the area somewhere as security checked his ID upon entrance. Heading towards Bandz he looked over his shoulders and noticed that the group of women was still behind him. Giving Bandz a hug soon as he approached her, he saw how one of the women looked at Bandz with jealousy in her eyes. "Don's in the bathroom." Bandz stated. While talking with Bandz Don Smoke returned and gave Kiem some dap as one of the women blew a kiss at him! Bold as shit, the woman demanded "Give me your number, I want you tonight!" Laughing at her aggressiveness, Don Smoke replied. "How 'bout you give me ya number, and we can further discuss ya wants! You feel me Ma?" He then asked. "Do I?" she replied. "By the way I'm Kola! I do apologize for being rude." "You good Ma! My name is Don, and it's a pleasure to meet you!" Writing her number down on a napkin, she handed it to Don Smoke then said, "Make sure you call me! Don't have me waiting on a ghost!" "I got you Ma!" He replied in a cocky but smooth way. Kiem and Bandz looked on with amazement knowing that Don Smoke could easily bag a chick with saying little to nothing! His style was suave for real! The group of women disappeared and did their own thing while Kiem, Bandz, and Don Smoke made ways towards the back elevators. Heading upstairs to the poker floors, Don Smoke and Bandz knew that Kiem was real good at reading his opponents when it came to the game! And the streetz was included! Buying in at $5,000, Kiem took a seat at the hold 'em table and challenged his opponents.

 Startled by the loud engine of a hoopty that drove by, Nicco woke up annoyed. Wiping the slob from the corner of his mouth, he pulled his self together and managed to make it inside the house. Smelling a foul stench he cursed like a sailor. "That stink ass shit! You could have at least turned the air conditioner on! All ya ass do is smoke. When the fuck you gonna get a job?! Crack head ass bitch!" Staggering up the stairs the smell got worst! You could smell the potency of the crack smoke still in the air, but you could also smell death too! It was a mixture that Nicco couldn't identify. His senses was all fucked up! Angry behind the smell, he continued to curse. "Dumb ass bitch! I got all these fucking brickz up in the attic, if somebody call the fire department, or some shit. I'm out back! A complete loss!" He said out loud while slamming his bedroom door. Too tired to do anything the Xanax took it's toll. Fully clothed with his boots still on, he laid back on his bed ready to fallout. As soon as his face hit the pillow he said "What the fuck is this wet fuzzy shit?" Rolling over to reach for the lamp, he clicked it on and damn near had a heart attack! Ahhh! He yelled out loud! In shock from the sight of a dead rat with its throat slit open, laid out on his pillow.

Still standing there dazed by the sight of a rat, about as big as a cat. Nicco grew torrid quick! Rushing into his mother's room, he instantly started vomiting as he bore witness to the horrific scene. The smell was so unbearable that it made his stomach turn upside down. Paranoia started to kick in, but he knew that he couldn't call 12 with all them brickz up in the attic. They would instantly yellow tape the entire house off then he would be in more shit. Constantly peeping out of the window, he racked his brain trying to figure something out. Maybe I can dispose of the body! He thought to himself. Time was ticking and he really didn't have much of a choice, as of what to do. "I have to get rid of this body!" He said out loud to himself. Not wanting to touch his own mother's disfigured dead body, he kicked her over while she was still duct taped to the chair. Trying to wrap the floor rug around her body and the chair, was a no go! Quickly he ran downstairs to the kitchen and grabbed a box of heavy-duty trash bags. Racing back upstairs. he tore the box open and removed several bags. Laying and laid them out on the floor. Nicco hurried and pulled loose the tape from around her wrist and ankles, then drug her body on top of the trash bags. The decaying body looked horrible. Her neck swung loose like a rope hanging from a tree. and it had razor wire wrapped tightly around it, well as her face. The smell had to be the worst of it all. Still he managed to try and wrap the body up in trash bags. With no luck, due to the stiffness of the corpse, he thought about chopping the body up. But it was too late for anything that would draw attention to the house. Looking around for something, anything, that would help him get rid of the body. He grabbed the sledgehammer from the corner and smashed down on his mother's shins. The sound of bones being cracked and crushed, was nerve wrecking. but time was something that wasn't on Nicco's side. Continuing his mission, he pounded the tool at her hips crushing them completely. Talking out loud to himself, while he pounded her rib cage and chest cavity. "Bitch! Won't nobody miss you! I don't know what you got ya self into but I'm not losing my stash just to bury ya crack head ass! Ya junkie ass wanna smoke, look at ya now! You're dead as fuck! Dead. You hear me?" Tired as fuck but he couldn't stop now. Grabbing what he could of the body, he managed this time to stuff it inside of the trash bag! He crushed the bones so bad, that he was able to stuff his mother's body inside of the trash bag with ease. Rolling the trash bag up inside of the floor rug. He quickly took the sheets off of the bed and tied off both ends of the rug. With the body now wrapped up, and ready for the garbage. Nicco rushed upstairs to the attic and retrieved the army duffle with the brickz and money inside. Heading straight out to his car he unlocked the door and tossed the duffle into his back seat. Opening his trunk, he looked around cautiously for anything that seemed to be watching him. Once he made sure everything was clear. He hurried back inside, then dashed upstairs and dragged the rug down the steps to the front door. Continuing to drag the rug outside of the front door, he picked the rug up on his shoulder, and carried it to his trunk! Slamming it down inside his trunk, he closed it immediately then got inside the car. Being more careful than he ever was in his life, he headed to the trash dump site hoping to discard of it before the early morning workers arrive. Nobody will discover the body there, and it'll be long gone before anybody knows that she's even missing. Nicco thought to himself.

Don Smoke and Bandz had the crowd of onlookers chanting Kiem's name, every time he won a pot. Up 70k, after only a few hands into the game, made Kiem realize what his connect told him earlier. "You give the orders and pull the strings." Thinking 'bout his status and knowing that he was far from finished with taking care of things, he folded his hand and sat back. The flop was revealed, then the river, and then the turn card. Smiling to himself, knowing that he folded a winner, but it didn't really matter! Right then and there he knew what his connect meant by saying. "You give the orders and pull the strings." Thinking to himself he said to underneath his breath.(if you don't go within, you go without). This was a jewel. Getting up from the table, he told the dealer to cash him out, as he looked back at Don Smoke and Bandz, then signaled for them to come. "Y'all ready to get up outta here?" Kiem asked. "We ready when you ready!' Bandz replied. "It's whatever my nigga!" Don Smoke stated. Counting his winnings out, another dealer then placed the money inside of a small size tote. then congratulated Kiem on his winnings. Now on the elevator going back downstairs to the first floor, Kiem handed Bandz the small tote, and told her to hold onto it for him! The elevator doors opened and the same group of women that followed Kiem into the casino, stood there in the lobby sipping on their drinks! Kola approached Don Smoke and said. "I'm coming with you for the night, so you don't even have to worry about calling me!" Taking him by his hand she then asked. "What we waiting for?" As her girlfriends waved her goodbye! "Go head my G! I want you to enjoy ya self! Everything that I want for me. I want for you! We gone build on things tomorrow. fo' sho! But for now. enjoy the moment my nigga!" Kiem sincerely expressed. "Say less my nigga! Besides I have to crack these nuts. Shit getting strenuous for a nigga!" Don Smoke stated. Walking through the main entrance, and out into the parking lot Kiem stated, "Oh yea! I gotta new toy, but it's more on the menu. We definitely gone build. Bandz you riding with me! Let bro do his thang!" "Fine with me nigga. How else was I gone get back?" Bandz asked. "Uhh! Uber?" Kiem said sarcastically. "You got jokes huh?" Bandz asked ready to fire at Kiem's ass. Approaching their cars, Don Smoke noticed the Panamera parked directly across from his and stated. "My nigga! That's what I'm talking 'bout! The Porsche is definitely you! Yo! Niggaz not even gone be able to ride this wave." Don Smoke stated. "Yo! Get up outta here! You got shorty standing at ya passenger door waiting on you!" Kiem stated. "Bros b4 hoez! My nigga!" Don Smoke stated seriously. "1lif my nigg!" Don Smoke said. Unlocking the doors Kiem and Bandz got inside of the Porsche. and just stared at each other. "Say something nigga! You all up in my shit. Don't act like ya ass can't get it!" Bandz stated in seductive tone of voice. "Ma! Yous a bad bitch. The whole city and cities outside of the city knows it! You're my ace and I respect you! My love for you is genuine because of the person that you are. We can flirt, look at each other ass naked, hold hands, even sleep in the same bed, and I still won't make a pass at you! My loyalty to you is greater than that! I will never be disloyal to you, or no one within our squad. Kiem explained. The Porsche drove smooth and was extremely fast. Eyeing Dons Audi from a distance. Kiem caught up to him within seconds but played the rear. Checking his mirrors, Don Smoke viewed Kiem's car a couple feet behind him. He already knew that Kiem was putting protection on him, following him to wherever he decided to go with Kola! Turning his

she stripped down to just her panties. Standing there in front of Don, she started to massage her breasts while swaying her hips side to side. Kola noticed his erection and smiled seductively at his imprint. "Come to me daddy!" She said lustfully while running her index finger in and out of her mouth. Standing face to face with Don Smoke, she instantly dropped down on her knees then released his baby leg from inside of his zipper! Handling him fully she grew extra excited by watching his facial expressions continuously change! Working her tongue all around his scrotum, she'd knew that it's been a minute since he'd last released himself! Feeling how tense he was, every time she allowed him deep into her mouth. she looked up at him with his pole still in position. Slowly releasing every inch of him, 'til his head was pressed firm against her lips! She nibbled on it gently then said, "I want you to juicy j me!" "Whaattt?" Don Smoke asked not understanding her lingo. "I want you to paint my face like a clown!" "Say less!" Don Smoke replied while grabbing her by the back of her head, making her gag and choke! Bobbing back and forth like she was at a carnival bobbing for apples, Don Smoke felt Mount Rushmore about to erupt! Holding her by her hair, he removed himself from her mouth as she closed her eyes and felt his candy rain all over her face and lips! "Paint me! Paint me!" She yelled out in pure ecstasy! I just created a masterpiece. he said to himself as he unloaded globs all on her face! Taking her panties off she rolled over onto her stomach, looked back at Don Smoke then said, "Come pound me! Make me hurt soooo good!" Without hesitation Don Smoke put on a Magnum and began banging on her drums!

Pacing the room floor back and forth Nicco kept peeping out the window and creeping up to the door looking through the peep hole. No doubt he was straight paranoid. And being too dumb founded, he had no idea of the danger that lurked or the situation that he got himself into. Still leaning off the Xanax, being 'noid wasn't making shit any better. The best thing he could do right now is to try and get some sleep. Placing the duffle bag on the floor, he hurried and pushed it underneath the bed. Then he put the chain lock on the door making sure that it was fully secure. Laying across the bed, he knew that he had to get him a weapon. Riding around with more coke than he ever imagined, and more money than he ever had, he knew that he was tripping moving without a weapon. The same way he got it; it was just that easy for the next nigga to take it! I gotta get me semi or something that'll knock a nigga dick in the dirt! He said to himself. Calling Keto's phone because he couldn't wait for tomorrow to come, he needed a gun now! "I know this nigga see me calling him!" Nicco said out loud angrily. Calling back to back and getting the same shit. Feeling his eyes get heavy, he dozed off into a deep sleep.

Back in the kitchen turning another 20 brickz into 60, Kiem's wrist was doing the most. Whipping like it was no tomorrow, beads of sweat dripped from his forehead, as he performed magic with the pots! Determined to meet his quota, he worked skillfully and quick, tripling the weight of each brick that he whipped. Thinking 'bout how everything took place Kiem wasn't gone rest 'til he put the whole puzzle together and fixed whoever involved that had something to do with it or anybody that got involved. With only 40 brickz left to whip, Kiem went and sat back on the recliner and kicked his feet up!

Scrolling through his phone he went to his messages and read the text that Bliss had sent. Not having time to read it when she sent it, he texted her back instantly. "In every way you are perfection and I respect your persona! Stay motivated, stay humble, most of all stay elevated! See you soon. XOXO Kiem." Remembering what Nice had said, 'bout some nigga getting dome checked in Lincoln Park. He went to his news feed to check out the breaking news report. "Fuckin' cops!" He said out loud to himself. "Always asking the community for help, but ain't got no fuckin' problem with shooting us down! Then they talk that you can remain anonymous bullshit for a cash reward." Thinking to himself, whoever the nigga was 12 hasn't contacted his next of kin yet, if they haven't released his name. Suddenly a rage filled his body like never before thinking 'bout how he was gone rip Nicco's guts out like a hysterectomy. The timing had to be perfect 'cuz it was no room for error. Knowing that this was something small compared to what still lies ahead, was the only thing that made Kiem turn straight savage! He already knew that this was far from the end, but it was the beginning of him securing his freedom. Getting up from the recliner he went into the back room of the den and pushed the bookshelf aside, then entered the combination on the wall safe. As the automatic steel door slid back revealing three gun shelves, he grabbed 2 Tech's with a few extensions, a Mac 11 with the muzzle on it, and a fisherman's hook knife. Kiem placed the weapons on the pool table then immediately closed the safe! Knowing that now was the time not to be moving with no hand guns, the big shit was on deck! Everything was semi being that Kiem knew what he was dealing with, and he knew that he had to mastermind his plan as well. With things figured out, him, Bandz and Don Smoke was gonna pay Hammer Time a little visit. "If Ms. Estelvo keeps lots of cash on deck, I'm taking everything. Every. Fuckin'. Thing! I'm 'bout to show this bitch what a savage is! Bandz know who the woman is that operates the front desk, and that's the bitch who knows the combination to the back office wall safe. It's crunch time!" Kiem said to himself then headed upstairs to the bedroom. Laying in bed staring up at the ceiling, he thought about everything from the beginning, and still couldn't figure out what it was that Ms. Estelvo wanted with him or from him. Closing his eyes, he needed some rest 'cuz he'd been up running, and it was either now or never with him getting some Zzz's!

Laid back in the driver's seat stuck in a heavy nod, Bo$$ heard Keto's phone ring. Just looking at it ring he was too caught up in his nod to even attempt to answer it. Thinking to himself, maybe it's that nigga who paid Keto all that cash and the brick, calling to see if the job was taken care of. Now scheming, Bo$$ put a plan together to work whoever the nigga was that's been calling Keto's phone. If it was the nigga calling that paid for the job, Bo$$ was gonna finesse dude for sure! Starting the MPV he drove off making his way back out to his lil freak bitch apartment. Bo$$ needed her to put a twist on things, and he would break her off a lil percentage! But she was gonna have to sell the nigga a dream, like he was a dead man sleep returning from the grave. Pulling up in front of his shorty building, he quickly parked and hopped outta the MPV, dashing into the building. Knocking at the door, he knocked. knocked. knocked. and knocked! No fuckin answer! He continued knocking on the door, until the knocks turned into loud bangs. Frustrated and angry he yelled "Stupid ass bitch! Open the fuckin door! I know ya coke head ass in there! Bitch if you don't open this door, I'm a kick it in. Then I'm a kick ya bald headed, no furniture having ass!" Kicking on the door, a few neighbors opened their door up to see what all the loud commotion was about. "Young man! Excuse me, young man! I'm going to have to call the police, it makes no sense you making all this wrecking!" An elderly woman angrily said. "Fuck you grandma and the police! This bitch won't open the door, fuck her ass too!" "I'm calling the police!" The elderly woman stated. Turning his back to leave the door suddenly opened. But Bo$$ continued walking, when his shorty ran out the door behind him and grabbed him by the arm. "Come on" she said while pulling on his arm. "Boy! Bring ya dumb ass before the police come!" She said in an annoyed tone of voice. Quickly making a u-turn, they both entered the apartment and the battle wars began! Bo$$ slapped fire from her ass knocking her to the floor. "Bitch what I tell you 'bout not opening the door when I come out here?" He furiously asked while standing over her. "Fuck you!" She said with all hostility in her voice as she kicked him in his dick. "You bittcchhh!!" He yelled out in pain. "I'm gonna beat ya thot ass!" Bo$$ stated seriously. "Ya dope fiend mommas the thot, bastard!" She said aggressively then jumped onto his back and did her best trying to choke him. "Yo! Fall back shorty. You got it, you got it!" Bo$$ pleaded. Still holding his dick, he just laid there on the floor balled up in a fetal position, praying for the pain to stop! "Bitch I was gone put you on to game, but ya ass so dumb I don't think I'm fucking with you on that level. You be bugging out doing some stupid ass shit. This shit is some real money shit, ya ass always be talking and you acting like a real bum bitch not wanting to open the fuckin door. Shorty you gotz to tighten the fuck up, if not I'm out!" Bo$$ explained. "Why the fuck you always get the say so, and get to do whatever the fuck you want, and I have to listen?" She asked. "Ya ass had me waiting for you all night, no show like usual! And you want me to act like everything's alright." She hurtfully expressed. "I've been on the block trying to take care of some shit, like I've already explained to you. Then I did like a half of bundle and I honestly zoned out! It ain't like I said fuck you intentionally. Bo$$ broke it down to her. "Besides it's some good as Dogg Food out my hood right now!" He stated. "What up with the coke?" She nosily asked. "That's what I was trying to explain to ya crazy ass! I know a nigga we can get but you got to put the spin game on him." Bo$$ explained. "Look! This what you do. When the nigga calls this phone that I got, you tell him that you're Keto's girlfriend. Tell him that the nigga got locked up out Irvington with some cocaine and money on him, but you don't know how much. Whatever it was, he don't have no bail right now. And you just had to get a ride to go pick his property up, he said if you called tell you that everything is stashed, but to call this number and take care of dude. He'll get you straight whenever they give him a bail." Bo$$ carefully explained. "You think you can handle this? You can't fuck this up! We pull this off, I got something for you!" He said in a serious, but greedy tone of voice. "I got you daddy. When are we supposed to do this?" She anxiously asked. "I got the phone right here." He said pulling it out of his pocket. "Soon as I recognize the number calling, you give ya best performance!" Bo$$ stated. "Okay Daddy! You still have more coke left?" Stroking her ego Bo$$ stated. "You know that I put something decent up for you. You always acting crazy and shit but you don't realize how much money we could be getting, instead of you always drawing unnecessary attention to us!" Bo$$ explained. "Baby! You know I don't be meaning no harm. I'm gonna do better, I promise!" She said in a soft remorseful tone of voice. Positioning her head at his groin area, she went to work like it was a nine to five!

After long minutes of pounding, Don Smoke replayed the scene over in his head, as Kola did her best to try and run from his strokes of death! Time was shaking fast. and Don Smoke wasn't trying to be laid up chillin', knowing that he had business to take care of. Heading towards the bathroom to take a quick shower. he stumbled upon Kola laid back in the tub with her eyes closed, enjoying herself. as he witnessed waves in the water from her hand going in a back and forth motion. Smiling to himself he proceeded to the shower and wash. Shit was epic whenever him and Kiem stepped out, their life was lit. And besides his brother from another and the squad; anybody could bleed! Loyalty was dying in the streetz! All the real niggaz was fading, while you had niggaz out in the streetz that was saluting bitch made niggaz! A nigga could get bagged, turn snitch, come home and niggaz a throw a party for him! Where they do that at? Don Smoke asked himself. Times had changed and it was a drought when it came to real niggaz! Thinking 'bout the jewel that Kiem had dropped on him. "One rise we all rise. Somebody fall hold 'em down. Somebody talk kill the rat, we can't leave room for no mice!" Either get out the way or get erased! Fuck all that homeboy shit knowing ya mans a rat! Grateful for having just one loyal nigga, amongst the rest of his squad, made all the work that he put in all worthwhile. But things were about to change heavily. Getting out of the shower, his thoughts continued heavy. Grabbing the towel to dry himself off, he noticed that Kola was watching him the whole time and paid her no mind. "Morning stranger!" Kola greeted him. "Good morning Ma! I see you enjoying the bath." Don Smoke said. "Of course! This was very much needed after such a remarkable time together." Kola expressed. "Glad to know that you enjoyed ya self!" He stated then headed back to bedroom. Quickly getting out of the tub, she followed behind him. No towel or nothing, as water dripped from her body, leaving wet imprints of her tiny feet on the carpet. Standing ass naked in front of Don Smoke, she asked. "Can I see you again?" "I believe we can arrange something!" He replied. Damn this bitch gotta nice body and the brains to go with it! He said to himself. Maybe something would develop between them he thought for a minute. But he was on a whole different side of the tracks, from that which she lived. Still if she was worth it, he would consider pursuing her. It's been plenty of nights where this type of shit jumped off, and the bitches were nothing more than jump offs! Even though Kola had a solid career, he knew that it could only work between them if she was loyal. Watching her as she got dressed was pure enjoyment to the eyes! Looking at her plump juicy ass wiggle, as she jumped into her jeans made him realize how super thick she was! Kola was sexy and beautiful! She definitely was a piece of arm candy for him. But he would have to put her on the back burner, knowing that it was more important things on the table right now to be taken care of. Fully dressed and ready to catch flight, Don Smoke asked Kola. "You hungry Ma?" "Not really. Some toast and a piece of fruit will do!" She replied. "You sure?" He asked. "I'm sure Don! Thanks for asking. I really appreciate your kindness!" "It's nothing Ma! You're also welcome!" He said in a sincere gentlemen's tone of voice. "If you want we can get you that toast and fruit from the waffle house." Don Smoke stated. "Thank you so much really, but the breakfast lounge downstairs is fine!" She said in an appreciative soft tone of voice. "Say no more then Ma! Just wanted to make sure you good!" He stated. "You're such a gentleman. I can't believe that you're single!" Kola said with excitement in her voice hoping that she might be able to have him. "Well let's say that we get up outta here!" She said. "Let's fly then Ma!" Taking her by the hand, they made way towards the door and exited.

Calling Bandz on speed dial, Gi-Gi already knew the count but was calling to let her know that The 7 Sexes, was all gonna meet up at the nail spa! Hearing her iPhone go crazy Bandz knew whoever it was calling had to be squad. She had no other reason to keep anyone else's number programmed in her shit. "What's goody bitch?" Bandz asked in an early morning grouchy tone of voice! "You know the count Ma! Just hittin' you up, to let you know that we all gonna meet up at the nail spa later today, 'bout five o'clock!" Gi-Gi stated. "No problem Gi-Gi. I should be back before then. Plus I gotta take my truck to get detailed. So what y'all gone do until then?" "Once we link up, we can all go get a bite to eat or something!" Gi-Gi stated. "I'm with that Ma! You know a bitch likez to eat!" Bandz said as her and Gi-Gi both laughed and hung up.

Getting up to grab something cold out of the fridge, Bandz made her way downstairs to the kitchen and noticed that Kiem been working. Shaking her head as she smiled to herself, she felt nothing but positive vibes this morning. knowing that it's always work to be done, no matter the situation. Deciding to help take a load off Kiem's hands, she took a seat and began breaking the boulders down. The tag and bag process wasn't nothing compared to whipping process, she thought to herself. Busy in the kitchen. Don Smoke made his presence known. "What's good Ma?" He asked then gave Bandz a hug before removing her gun from his waistline and handing it to her. "You know what's good nigga! You all happy and shit! Somebody got their lil man wet!" She said sarcastically as she laughed. "Ya ass funny you know that?" Don Smoke asked. "Don't get sentimental on me nigga damn!" She stated. Don Smoke couldn't do nothing but laugh! Bandz was one of the realest, flyest, most loyal females he'd ever met, and she was all the way with the bullshit! "What da fuck is so funny?" She asked sounding annoyed. "Nothing is funny Ma! Your energy is so great that you really add that spark to a nigga world!" "Thankz Don!" "You welcome Ma! Look I gotta go get this money out the box right quick. Afterwards we gone build on some things!" Don Smoke said. "I'm all ears nigga!" Bandz replied.

Waking up paranoid as fuck Nicco still kept peeping out the window and creeping up to the door, looking through the peephole. Shit was starting to get stressful for him but he had to maintain his composure! "I gotta get in touch with Keto and see what the fuck is going on. Plus I need that nigga to get me some protection, and handle the arson for me. I have to get in touch with this mutha fucka!" He said loud.

"Bo$$. Bo$$. Wake the fuck up! That phone is ringing!" Shorty stated anxiously. Stuck in his nod and barely moving. She remembered what Bo$$ had told her but didn't know if this was the person calling or not so she took a chance. Swiping the answer icon on the screen, she listen as the caller went the fuck off! "Nigga! Why the fuck you haven't been answering the phone? Did you and mans even take care of that situation? Yo! You fucking up big time, and I threw you a whole extra chicken on top of the fifty thousand. Nigga everything better be done or that's your ass! You hear me talking? Yo! Why the fuck you ain't saying shit?" "Hello!" She said. "Who the fuck is this?" Nicco snapped. "This is Keto's wifey mutha fucka!" She replied than gave the performance of the year! "May I ask who this is calling?" "Tell him it's Nicco!" Quickly putting two and two together from what he said when she first answered the phone she started to finesse Nicco. "Nicco. Keto said if you called to let you know what's going on! He got arrested out Irvington with some drugs and cash on him, I don't know how much to be exact but he don't have no bail right now! Bad enough I had to scramble to find a ride just to go pick his property up! He said not to worry, everything is in the stash and he got you once he gets a bail. He also gave me a number to give you, he said to make sure that you take care of his peeps! The number is 917-1017. He said to call soon as possible, they're expecting your call." She explained while smiling mischievously. "No problem. Let him know to call me if he needs anything!" Nicco stated. "I'll be sure to tell him." She replied then hung up! "Bo$$! Bo$$! Get the fuck up now! You all high the fuck up and we supposed to be making a money move." Shaking him vigorously he started to come up out of his baby coma. "What! What! Whaattt!!" He angrily yelled. "Somebody name Nicco just called that phone looking for Keto!" Hearing Keto's name bought him back to his senses immediately! "What you say? What you tell the nigga? Why you ain't get me the fuck up?" Bo$$ nervously asked. "Nigga I've been trying to get ya ass up for the longest! You the one doped up out of ya fuckin' mind! But I took care of shit like you explained to me. I told him dude got knocked and left a number for him to call to make sure you take care of his peeps! Then I gave the nigga ya number. so be expecting a call. I did my part the rest is up to you now!" She explained. "Did he seem like he was buying the storey?" Bo$$ asked. "You better believe he was!" She stated nonchalantly. "Good looks shorty! We 'bout to be on now!" Bo$$ said greedily. "Go grab that backpack out of my van! Don't go in it or I'm not gonna give ya ass nothing!" Bo$$ said. "Nigga please!" She stated.

Now super paranoid more than ever, he didn't know what to think, nor who to trust! Thinking to himself that nigga might tell on me if he got a distribution charge. Who knows what he got caught with, or how much money he had on him! But what I do know is how the interrogation room works! Talk and you walk! It's that simple. But it ain't like he got bagged with a few brickz, shit. If he mention my name about anything, I'm just gonna push that shit off on Kiem's ass! Fuck a nigga think? I'm not going to jail for nobody. It's a dirty game but you gotz to be more careful! Looking at the number that he wrote down he wondered to himself, if it was the number to the lil nigga that ran with Keto. Hoping that it was, 'cuz he needed the lil nigga to handle some shit for him. I'll just throw the lil nigga a whole chicken to handle the arson, and to knock Bliss off! Either way I'm still winning! He said to himself in a cocky tone of voice. After moments of debating with himself, he decided to call the number. Watching shorty walk around ass naked, she really did have a nice size ass! Her titties wasn't so big, but they wasn't too

garage and put 'em in ya trunk. It's already a box of latex gloves, ski masks, and vests inside." Kiem explained. "Once we do this Don Smoke, you take off and we'll meet you here!" "Copy!" Don Smoke replied. "Other than that watch for my signals at Main Event, that's the key to move!" "Already!" Bandz and Don Smoke replied. "Where's that cash from last night Ma?" Kiem asked. "Oh shit! It's still in ya car! I left it. Not intentionally though! Let me get it right quick!" Within a few seconds she was back with the small tote in her hand. Handing it to Kiem, he then dumped it out onto the table, and divided the money 3 ways equally, then divided the last 10 thousand between Bandz, and Don Smoke, giving Bandz and Don Smoke both 25 thousand each! They asked what's the money was for? Saluting them both he said "Go buy something nice. Main Event tomorrow. Drippy, drippy!" Giving Kiem a big long hug, Bandz thanked him from the bottom of her heart! "Aight Ma! You can let me go now!" "Nigga thatz dead. I'll let you go when I'm ready to!" She said sarcastically while hugging on him tighter! Don Smoke laughed his ass off, 'cuz Bandz always fucked with Kiem. She was down for the count and she genuinely loved him to death! "Let's get ready to bounce!" Kiem stated. "I do have an nail appointment with my bitches! So let's get ghost!" Bandz stated. "Don keep y'all handguns in the box, along with the Tec and the Mac!" Kiem stated. "Once we dip I'll get with y'all at Main Event! Also, Bandz take three of those boulders to Gi-Gi. Make sure that she knows it's 9 brickz total. That will hold the Sexes down until the heat dies down 'cuz it's 'bout to be scorching!" Kiem explained. Reaching underneath the kitchen counter, Kiem grabbed two brown paper bags and quickly began putting the money that Don Smoke had counted out from the runs inside. Bandz hurried and stashed all the recent tags and bags inside of the ottoman with the other 15 brickz. While Don Smoke went down to the garage and stashed the guns inside the box! Everything was straight and the squad was ready to hit the interstate. Shaking hands with his bro he then gave Bandz a tight ass bear hug, as the bones in her back cracked! "Main Event. Love y'all!" Kiem stated then got inside the Porsche and started the engine! Slowly pulling outta the garage Don Smoke followed suit before taking off in his own direction.

Parked on Broad St, watching multiple cars ride by and none of them parking, Nicco gave it as few more minutes before he decided to make the call. Parked directly in front of an all Black Challenger with dark tint made it look like he was riding two cars deep for real! Watching as an old raggedy ass MPV pulled up and parked across the street from the Red HellCat! Nicco said to himself this has to be that nigga! Calling the young niggaz phone, "I'm out here." Bo$$ said as he answered his phone. "Where you at?" Bo$$ asked. "Don't walk up to the Black Challenger, come to the passenger's side of the red HellCat parked in front of it!" Nicco explained. "Coming now. I'm in the Dark Blue MPV!" Bo$$ replied. "Hand me that backpack!" He said to his shorty. Removing the 38 special from the backpack. Bo$$ tucked it inside his waistline, then got out the MPV and walked over to the HellCat. Opening the door, Bo$$ got inside of the HellCat then introduced himself. "I'm Bo$$!" he said extending his hand. Nicco shook the young nigga hand then introduced himself "I'm Nicco." "What's the dealy?" Bo$$ asked. "It's simple. This address. Go there and gasoline the whole fuckin' place! Turn the gas on and everything. Make sure that the house burns down! The front door is already unlocked, but

I need this taken care of tomorrow night after 1:00am." Nicco stated. Opening the piece of paper, Bo$$ read the address then said "I know exactly where this street is in Jersey City!" "Good!" Nicco replied. "You got that hammer I asked you about?" "Indeed." Bo$$ said as he pulled the black 38 from his waistline. Wiping it off with the bottom of his T-shirt, he then placed the gun in Nicco's hand. "What you want for this?" Nicco asked. "I would've only charged you $500, but now I'm a be out here ass naked. So I gotz to charge you a stack." Bo$$ said. "You got bullets for it?" Nicco asked. "Open it up, it already got four slugs inside." Bo$$ said. "This shit ain't gonna jam on me, is it?" Nicco asked. "Hell no! It's a revolver my nigga! These shitz never ever jam!!" Bo$$ stated in a cocky ass tone of voice! Reaching into his pocket, he took out the thousand dollars he counted earlier and handed the money to Bo$$. "Now that we took care of that situation, what's up with this bitch you want murdered?" Bo$$ asked. "The bitch name is Bliss! Pretty mutha fucka with long wavy jet black hair. The bitch hair comes past her ass then some. She drives a purple 550SL coupe. You can't miss her. When you see this bitch she's definitely a head turner! But the bitch has to go A.S.A.P." Nicco explained. "Where do I locate the bitch at?" Bo$$ asked anxiously. "That's the thing! You just gonna have to be on the look out for her whip then hit the bitch up!" Nicco stated. "I'm following you so far! So how fast do you need this job taken care of?" Bo$$ asked. "Like yesterday!" Nicco replied. "Alright then. I'm on it! Where's my payment?" Bo$$ asked. Reaching under his driver's seat, he pulled out the plastic bag and handed it to Bo$$. "When you handle this job, I got a lil something extra for you! Call me!" Nicco stated. "It will be taken care of with the quickness!" Bo$$ said. Getting out of the HellCat, Bo$$ made his way back to the MPV got inside and turned the ignition then drove off! "We did it shorty. We did it!" Bo$$ said excitedly. "I have to handle a lil business for dude, something small tomorrow night. Then I have to put in some work! I'll tell you about it later." Bo$$ said. "But for now we about to go have a lil fun! Don't think I forgot about you because ya ass is about to get paid too! I need you to work these jobs with me! Okay?" Bo$$ explained. "I hear you nigga! I'll believe it when I see it!" She said. "See what?" He asked. "My pay mutha fuckin' negro!" She exploded. "You'll see soon as we get back to our spot!" He said. "Oh! Now it's our spot huh!" She said sarcastically. "Relax. I got you! You know I got you!" He stated. "We'll see! What's in the plastic bag?" "It's a fortune of a lifetime!" Bo$$ said greedily. Parking in front of his shorty apartment building, they got out of the MPV and hurried into the building. Sitting on her double stacked mattress, which laid on the floor without a box spring, Bo$$ dumped the contents of the small white plastic bag, onto the bed. Her eyes almost bulged out of its sockets while looking at the brick shaped package wrapped in plastic. "How much is all of that?" She asked Bo$$. "It's a whole brick!" He replied. "A brick?" She had asked dumbfounded. "A kilo shorty, one kilo!" He explained. "So we rich now right?" She asked. "We gotta move the shit first, which is nothing!" He stated. Pulling the backpack from between the mattress he took the coke out that was inside. He took the mirror that was hanging on the wall and placed the coke on it and started digging into what was left with a butter knife. He split it in half and slid the biggest portion of it across the mirror over to her. "Here. This is your half. Do what you want with it!" He said in a non caring way. "What about the stuff you just got?" She greedily asked. "I'm selling every gram of it. We need the fucking money!" He said in a stern tone of voice. "That's not fair. That shit ain't even right, and you know it ain't!" "Look I just gave ya strung out ass a whole half of kilo. What part of we need the money you not understanding?" He angrily asked. "Don't even worry about it! You handle shit by ya self mutha fucka!" She said angrily. "Bitch I'm not! You must be out ya rabbit ass mind if you think I am!" He arrogantly screamed. "You know what. I got ya rabbit! You dope fiend bitch!" She said in a hurtful tone of voice. "I know what you did so keep running ya fuckin mouth!" She said in a stern but cocky tone of voice. Looking at the bitch, he didn't know if she knew anything or not! But what he did know is that she had to go! Bo$$ didn't play the police game, and didn't fuck with no bitch that made threats with 12. Bottom line she had to go! Wasn't no coming back from this! "I'm about to make a few runs, gotta see if it's any money coming through the hood! But we gonna do us later, I got something nice for you too! What size dress you wear?" He asked. "You know I'm a size small." She answered. "Why?" "I seen something I want you have. Besides I want you to go out in style when we step out!" He said acting like he cared. "Take a bath and get ya self together. I'll be back in a few!" He said then left out the door.

Walking through the Garden State Plaza, Nicco made a few stops and picked up some designer. He never owned nothing Tom Ford and decided to cop a raw denim jean suit. Looking at the mannequin in the Gucci store window, he went inside and purchased the Gucci Chuck Taylor's, along with the matching belt, shirt, and hat. Feeling like he's the shit he walked into the Diamond District and purchased a white gold Cuban link chain with an iced out money bag medallion. With his new attire in hand, he made way towards the mall exit, and out into the parking lot! Throwing the bags into his trunk, he pulled off in route back to the hotel.

Coming off the turnpike, Don Smoke drove Bandz straight to the nail spa and dropped her off. Waving to Gi-Gi and the rest of the Sexes, as he waited for Bandz to put the 3 boulders inside of a small laundry tote. They all blew kisses at him, while XL stuck her tongue out at him. Shaking his head at their wild gestures, Don Smoke knew that it was all love. Giving Don a hug as she got out the car she said to him. "Get withcha tomorrow! You know the count!" as she shut the passenger's side door. "Already" he replied then drove off! Now on his way home. Don Smoke couldn't wait to hit the bed and just rest! After all it was back to basics come shortly.

Slumped over the toilet, Bliss wasn't feeling good at all. She felt like straight shit and been running a slight fever. Vomiting again, she couldn't stand the nasty acidic taste it left in her mouth! Managing to get herself up, she flushed the toilet and then brushed her teeth. The garage door opened as Kiem pulled in and parked right next to Bliss' Benz. Sliding the ashtray out, he removed the ring that he put there. Looking at the ring he felt like he would be doing his connect a disservice, if he did not wear it in honor of all that he'd accomplished. From that moment on, Kiem would never remove the ring again, once he put it back on. Grabbing the two paper bags of money, he got out the car and entered the house. Disarming the alarm system, then resetting it once he was inside alerted Bliss that he was home! So excited that he was home she couldn't control herself. Walking into their bedroom, Bliss instantly jumped into his arms and placed her head on his shoulder! Still holding both paper bags and Bliss at the same time, he made it over to the bed and sat her down. "Damn Ma! You hot as hell! What you sick? You feel like you got a fever!" He said in a concerned tone of voice. "I knowww! I've been feeling like shit for the last few days!" She said in a slurred manner. "You go to the doctor?" He asked. "Noooo." She stubbornly replied. Kiem knew how she was so it was no use trying to talk her into going. Instead he played doctor and took care of her for the brief time that he would be home. "Listen, I have some important shit to handle tomorrow, and I'm back on the road." Sucking her teeth she asked. "Why you can't stay with me for a few days?" Feeling bad 'cuz he knew she wasn't feeling well and that she needed him he decided to send for her as soon as he got back. "Ma, soon as I get back I will send for you. You can come spend a few days with me!" "Alright!" Smiling like never before her eyes started to tear up as she reached for him and wrapped her arms around his neck tight as ever. "You and Bandz gone stop with these tight ass hugs!" He said playfully trying to make her laugh. "I'm about to make us some grilled cheese and shop! Then we can watch any one of our favorite movies." He stated. "Oohhh! Oohh! City of God, bae. Please." "Anything for you my Queen!" He said.

Up in the nail spa, The Seven Sexes was getting all glamorous like usual, anticipating tomorrow night! Rose XL couldn't wait to walk through the main entrance and stop everything moving! She despised Nicco and wanted nothing more than to slap his teeth out of his fucking mouth! Just talking 'bout that nigga angered her. With everyone almost finished they all agreed to hit the Panda Express afterwards for a bite to eat.

Leaving out of the convenient store, Bo$$ had his purchase in a small paper bag and moved carefully as time was ticking. It was getting late, and he knew that once darkness approached he would have to make his move, or forever hold his peace!

Enjoying the movie, grilled cheese sandwiches and tomato soup, Bliss laid snuggled up under Kiem. Dozing off, she drifted off into her own world, with expectations of just them. Hitting Nice on speed dial, Kiem paused the movie and turned to the news. "What's good lil bro?" Nice asked answering the phone. "You already know my nigga! Just touching base with you." Kiem stated. "Everything Gucci where y'all at?" Nice asked. "No doubt! Just shaking and moving, getting' to that bag! Ya ass should come out there sometimes and flex!" Kiem stated. "Mann!! If I ain't have to be here to run the club, you know I'll be out there with you!" Nice replied. "Yo! You ain't never think about opening another club?" Kiem asked. "Nah, not now. Why what's up?" "I'm sayin' we can network in different places on a level that niggaz can't reach at different speeds. Feel me?" Kiem expressed. "I feel you my nigga! Imma stay open to that opportunity though. If things present itself then we get the ball moving!" Nice explained. "Yo, they talking 'bout that body that was found in Lincoln Park on the news right now!" Kiem said. "27 year old Keto Mansum. Bro! I know that name from somewhere. I can't put my finger on it right now! But I recognize that name!" Kiem explained with all seriousness in his voice. "I'm thinking too and if I'm not mistaken that's the nigga who use to run with Nicco soft ass!" Nice stated. "That's it! I knew that I knew that name."

Kiem said. "Whatever he did a nigga fixed his ass!" Kiem stated. Left him out back! Nice replied. Bro! Ya ass crazy and mutha fuckaz wonder where I get it from! Love dat nigga." Kiem expressed. "Love you too lil bro! Catch you at the club!" Nice replied. "One!" Kiem stated. Then their lines went dead. Kiem walked to the bathroom where he had his money and drugs stashed at. He took 10 brickz and brought it back into the bedroom with him. Thinking to himself this should hold Nice down 'til the heat dies down and I get back! He then got undressed and hopped in the bed with Bliss.

Pulling back up in front of who use to be his shorty apartment building. He put the small paper bag inside of his pocket and grabbed the H&M shopping bag. Hurrying into the building, this was the moment of truth for him. Knocking on the door, she opened it this time without hesitation. Seeing the shopping bag in his hand, she played her part knowing that it was for her. "Hey Daddy! You really did come back this time!" She said happy as ever. "I told you that I would be back with something nice for you." He said mischievously. "Here this is for you. Go get dressed while I bag some coke up!" "Okay Daddy!" She said then vanished into the bathroom. Once he heard the water start running, he knew that he had to move with the quickness. Grabbing the mirror, he took the paper bag out of his pocket and removed the box of rat poison. Quickly breaking off an ice cube size piece of coke, he opened the box of rat poison and dumped it onto the mirror. Quickly mixing the two together, he smiled like the joker. She came out of the bathroom with the all Black fitted H&M dress on. "How do I look?" She cheerfully asked. "You look like ya going to a place where you ain't coming back." Bo$$ said in a wicked tone of voice. Not catching his drift, she thanked him then greedily asked. "You gonna give me something? I didn't touch what you gave me. I'm gonna let you take care of things!" She said sounding like she had a wake up call. "Here you go right there!" Bo$$ said pointing to the mirror. Taking the end piece of a Newport box, she instantly went skiing. "Whooo! This coke is damn near raw. This is the best shit I've ever had!" She said before taking another hit. Suddenly she looked at Bo$$ and started going into convulsions. Her body started twisting and jerking as she started foaming from the mouth. Struggling for help she reached out to him but stumbled to the floor, as he kicked her in the face calling her all types of bitches! After a few minutes, the struggle was over. Her helpless body just laid there, stretched out on the floor. "You stupid dumb bitch! Betcha ass won't send indirect police threats no more!" He said in a harsh tone. Taking back the coke that he had given to her earlier, he tossed it into the backpack, then exited the apartment.

Finally the weekend was here! It was now Friday and just like any other Friday, all the clubs would be flooded, the streetz would be packed, and there would be plenty of money to be made. Waking up Kiem looked at Bliss knowing that he had moves to make. He didn't want to leave her during her time of sickness, but he had to. Kissing her on the cheek, he got up and showered. Pulling into Bubble & Glitz, Bandz went through the same shit, every time she pulled up to her truck detailed. "Nooo Henry!" She said in a sarcastic tone. The old Puerto Rican man stayed trying his best to make Bandz his Mamacita. The old man said smiling. "Ye beautiful Mi' Amor!" "Gracias!" Bandz laughed shaking her head at him. He was a very nice old man, she thought to herself! But he wasn't for her at all. He had a pot belly like Santa Claus and was very short with a

Mario Bros mustache. But he worked his ass off and Bandz respected that about him. He made her G-Wagon look showroom floor new every time she came through. Bandz paid the $60.00 detailing fee, plus tipped Henry $300. "Gracias! Gracias! Mi Amor!" He said gladly. "See you next time Henry." Bandz stated.

At the barber shop gettin' a light fade, Shark couldn't wait to catch Nicco's ass, as he thought to himself about how he was gonna embarrass him in front of everybody! Talking to his barber 'bout things. "Maannn! That'z some slime shit there Shark!" His barber stated. "Who you telling! I was feeding the nigga bruh! He'd supposed to have been my nigga but he allowed some pussy to come between us! Then I'm hearing he's plugged now and the nigga ain't even bother to hit me up, or nothing! Ain't check to see if I was good or nothing!" Shark expressed. "You know I've been hearing the same thing 'bout him being plugged. But I haven't been seeing him lately. Maybe that's the reason why nobody's been seeing, or hearing from him." His barber stated. Finishing up, he then got out of the chair and paid his barber for the cut. Making his way out to his car he seen Nicco's 370z, ride past. "There his bitch ass go right there!" He said out loud to himself as he got into the Beamer and drove off. Barbershop gossip spread quick. It was the one place where anybody that had anything to do with the streetz, could stay in tuned with the latest!

Bandz sat back with her head under the drier as she let the hair dye dry. Listening to her hair stylist and another stylist talk, she overheard them discussing how Shark was beefing with Nicco behind him fucking Cheebah. She really didn't care about the beef part, nor the fact that Cheebah was doing what thotz do, she focused on the fact that Shark will surely be at Main Event, trying to spin on Nicco. That would take all the attention off what Kiem and her had in line! The drier stopped and Bandz sat up, looked in the mirror, and smiled. Happy with her new hair style, she decided that it would be her signature look from now on! Counting out five blue faces, she handed it to her hair stylist, then thanked her! "You're welcome Bandz! But you really didn't have to do this." Her stylist stated. "It's nothin'! You really do deserve it for ya time and skillz!" Bandz replied. Exiting the salon Bandz hit Kiem ASAP. "What's good Ma?" He asked answering the phone. "Nigga! I just left da salon right? Tell me why I overheard that Shark is beefin' with Nicco behind him fuckin' Cheebah!" Bandz stated. "Get the fucckkk outta here!" Kiem replied. "You know what that means right?" He asked Bandz. "You betta believe I do!" She replied. "Everything is still as planned, I'll catch you tonight!" Kiem said. "Already!" Bandz replied then hung up. His phone started ringing again. "Talk to me." he stated as he answered the phone. "How are you my good friend?" His connect asked. "Everything is well." Kiem replied. "Good! Good! Your shipment will be where you demanded at the approximate time! Remember to keep the vision black until you're ready for use." His connect explained. "I understand!" He replied. "Very well then my friend!" As both their lines went dead. Noticing the ring on his pinky finger, as she opened his eyes! Bliss complimented the jewel. "Nice ring you got there!" "Thanks! So how are you feeling?" He asked concerned. "Not too much different, I just need to rest." she said. "You need to go see a doctor. You might have a stomach virus or something!" Kiem expressed. "I might." She said sounding doubtful. "Look I'm gone get Gi-Gi to go

parking lot stopped whatever they were doing, as the silver chromed out Porsche pulled up. Don Smoke and Bandz, stood side by side smiling 'cuz they knew who it was! Kiem seen the hate in niggaz eyes, as he drove by and pulled into a parking space. All the bitches were busy breaking their neck, focusing on his drip as he drove by not really paying attention to who was driving the Porsche. Getting out of the Panamera, his neck, wrist, and pinky, lit up the parking lot. Factz! Making his way over to Don Smoke and The 7 Sexes, Kiem dapped his main man up, then gave each of the Sexes a hug and kiss on the cheek. "Kiem I love that Porsche! I know you gone let me push that!" Gi-Gi said with excitement in her voice. "You know you can whip it anytime you want Ma!" He replied. "Yea Kiem! I gotz to go for a ride in the Porsche!" Rose XL stated. Whyte Diamonds, Passion Shooter, Storemy, and N.D.A., all wanted to take pictures on the hood of the Porsche. Don Smoke started snapping pics of The Sexes on his phone as Bandz and Gi-Gi joined in. Bandz then grabbed Kiem and pulled him into group, as The 7 Sexes did the most. Hate didn't even matter 'cuz problems in their city been deaded! Entering the club, the squad already had 18 bottles waiting on them at their VIP section. Eyeing Nicco, Kiem monitored his every move. Approaching Gi-Gi and Bandz, Nicco sat down to talk, while he ordered 3 bottles. "This is a nice party Nicco!" Gi-Gi stated. "So what's this shit 'bout you moving for the low?" "Simple. I know you copping work from Kiem, and I know his prices! I also been copping from him 'til I ran across a connect. Now I can move at a much better rate with good product too!" Nicco arrogantly stated. "And what you call a much better rate?" Gi-Gi asked. "I'm talkin' 30k flat!" Nicco replied. "How we know if this shit you got is even worth 30k?" Bandz asked. "Tell you what! I'll throw y'all a brick for 20k right now so y'all can see the results once y'all put it out on the streetz!" Nicco replied. "A whole brick for 20k right now?" Gi-Gi asked. "That'z right!" Nicco replied. "So if you gonna do that, I know we can get 3 for 50k! That'z if you really want our business and want us to stop buying from Kiem!" Bandz stated. "I'll do that for y'all this time around. After this round. it's 30k! Kool?" "That'z fine! But you forgettin 'bout da real business. How u gonna try to tax a bitch, and expect me to be ya girl?" Bandz asked. "You know I'm not gonna tax you for nothing once we get shit situated!" Nicco replied. "Nigga you must think I'm sum lame ass bitch or something!" Bandz screamed at him. "Nah! Nah! It's nothing like that!" Nicco pleaded. "It ain't huh?" Bandz questioned before putting a lil pressure on him. "Look! What you tryna do? You act like you don't know what time it is! You talkin' all dis money shit. I needs to know what ya pocketz talkin' 'bout nigga! 10k ain't even enough for me to talk dirty to you! You gotta up ya dollaz if you want me to holla." Bandz said in a calm seductive tone of voice. Looking at her ass in that cat suit made him wanna throw a couple thousand at her. "Imma take care of you as long as you take care of me! We both win at the end of the night!" Nicco stated while staring at her erect nipples. "What time you tryna bounce, so we can go do us?" Bandz asked. "Relax for a bit and let me handle a few things, then we can bounce! Aight?" "If you say so nigga!" Bandz stated in a bossy tone of voice. Signaling for a waitress at the bar, one approached Nicco, as he told her to take 2 bottles over to Kiem's VIP section. He then tipped her a hundred dollar bill. Doing as she was told the waitress bought two bottles over to Kiem's VIP section, and said that Nicco sent them! Looking in Nicco's direction, Kiem rejected the bottles then said out loud across the sections, "No new friends!" Then he tossed his own bottle back!

Conversations with selected crowds made Nicco feel on top of the world as he was setting up distribution deals for the low! Seeing Shark walk up in the club let Kiem know that it was 'bout to go down! Moving through the crowd he spotted Nicco and pulled up on him with the quickness. Kiem made a signal with his right thumb and pinky finger as Bandz slid off without no one even noticing that she was gone. Heading out the club's back exit she hurried around the front of the parking lot and snatched her bag up outta her G-Wagon, then got behind the wheel inside of Kiem's car. Don Smoke followed suit and waited in the R8 'til Kiem came outside. Grabbing Nicco by the back of his shirt collar, Shark turned him around and punched him dead in his jaw! Nicco hit the floor quick, trying to get back up on his feet. But Shark wasn't letting up! The punches came rapidly, followed by a few kicks! The entire club stood in silence as they watched what use to be, two grimy niggaz that rocked with each other, go at one other! Big Dream and a few other bouncers broke the squabble up and kicked them both out of the club. Everybody knew why the fight took place, but for those that didn't they would soon find out. Shark started yelling at Nicco. "Yous a bitch nigga! You was fucking Cheebah the whole time and you ain't even let me know! That's what this shit is about!" Nicco replied. "I got you nigga, I got you! Wait 'til we get outside!" Nicco threatened Shark. "Oh! You gangsta now? Since when?" Shark sarcastically asked. Nicco got tossed out the club first and Shark was right behind. Immediately, Shark ran to his Beamer and grabbed a 9mm then started licking shots at Nicco. Pop! Pop! pop. pop. pop! Hitting everything besides Nicco, Shark shot out niggaz car windows, and put holes in the driver's side door of a niggaz Benz! From out of nowhere Nicco let the 38 loose! Boom! Boom! Boom! Boom! Click. Click. Click. Click! Click! "Fuck!!" He yelled out as he had no more shots! He did manage to hit Shark in his upper leg! Feeling like a real gangsta, he hopped in the HellCat, and sped off. Following right behind him, Shark let off a few rounds out of his driver's side window. Still no luck, as the HellCat moved with speed and power dipping through the streetz! Don Smoke eased up a few feet behind Nicco's car, keeping an eye on him. While Shark reared off down another street, as sirens was heard from a distance! Bandz pulled up right beside Don Smoke. while Kiem was ghost riding the whip. The Porsche was the truth and Bandz loved the way it drove! The light just turned red and it was now or never. Pushing the Panamera she slid up on the passenger's side of Nicco's car and looked at him before getting out and getting into the car with him. "What you just gonna leave ya whip like that?" He asked. "It's a rental. Fuck it! They'll recover it!" Bandz said nonchalantly! "I was worried 'bout you! You got me out here at ya party and all this crazy shit goin' on." She said sounding angry. "I'm sorry, but that nigga just jealous!" "What da fuck was that shit 'bout anyway?" Bandz asked playing dumb. "That nigga mad cuz his bitch is a thot! That bitch a fuck anybody for some paper. Anybody!" Nicco stated. "Who? Cheebah?" Bandz asked. "Yea! That's the bitch name!" Nicco replied harshly. Turning her game all the way up Bandz knew the location was coming. Jumping straight into his lap while he was driving made him nervous, as Bandz started to wine her hips in a slow circular motion, while whispering in his ear! "It feelz good don't

it? You think you can handle this pussy? Can you fuck me, like I've always dreamed of
you doin'? Huh?" She asked aggressively as she started to bounce slowly in his lap.
Feeling what she thought was him getting erect, she wanted to laugh bad as shit. Pencil
dick was the only thing that ran through her mind. Too shook to talk all he could do was
nod his head, knowing that he was about to fuck the shit out of Bandz sexy ass! Turning
on a back street, Bandz didn't even have to tell him. It was like he already knew where
his death sentence would been held. Pulling up in front of the Steak City Warehouse,
Nicco thought that this would be the best blind spot to fuck Bandz. "Let's get in the back
seat!" Bandz stated. Climbing over the seat first, she took her time knowing that Nicco
would want to fondle her. Grabbing on her soft thick ass Nicco then reached between her
legs, and felt how hot her pussy was. Smelling his hand he replied. "Damn! Your pussy
smells good! Let me eat you." "Not so fast Trick Daddy! What's up with my money?"
Bandz asked. "I got you, I got like 80 plus brickz in the trunk, and over $200k in cash!"
Nicco stated in a stern but cocky tone of voice. "Nigga! You better not be playin'! And
I'm dead ass!" She replied. "Don't worry! Let Nicco take care of you!" He said. Burying
his face between her legs, he attempted to eat her out through her lace cat suit. This nigga
is desperate as fuck! She said to herself. "Hold up. Let me take my suit off!" Before you
know it Kiem and Don Smoke was standing at the driver's side, and passenger's side
door of Nicco's car with their guns aimed at him! "Get ya fucking bitch ass out the car
now!" Kiem said snatching the door open and pulling him out of the car! Holding him by
his collar, Kiem walked him up the loading ramp and into the doors of the warehouse.
"Yo! What's goin' on? What the fuck you tripping for?" Nicco nervously asked Kiem.
"Shut the fuck up until I tell you to talk!" Kiem said in a calm smooth tone of voice.
Walking towards the back of the warehouse Bandz came with the two Tyvek suits, as
Don Smoke lowered the hook chains. "Don, hold this nigga right quick. If he even blink
his eye wrong, head shot!" Kiem commanded. As him and Bandz put on their Tyvek
suits. Nicco knew that he'd better tell 'em whatever it was that they wanted to know, or
his ass was gone! Grabbing Nicco up, Bandz gagged his mouth as Kiem dragged him
over to the hook chains. "This ain't gone hurt but a little bit as long as you don't struggle
or resist." Kiem stated then lifted Nicco up off his feet, as Bandz held open his arms and
then dropped him down on the hooks! The hooks were so sharp that they instantly
pierced through his arms! One hook up under his left armpit, and another hook up under
his right armpit! Blood gushed from under his armpits like running water! Nicco couldn't
yell or nothing 'cuz Bandz had the nigga mouth roped up! All he could do is squirm like a
piece of meat on the hooks, knowing it was about to be slaughtered. "Mutha fucka! Look
at me!" Kiem demanded. "Look at me! And you better hold ya fucking head up! All that
money you been running around spending! That was my fucking money! All that coke
you'd been running around moving for the low! That was my fucking coke! That safe that
you emptied out! That was my fucking safe! Those 3 brickz that you got caught with! I
know about the statement that you gave, you rat bastard! The foreign bitch that you've
been doing business with, she's been using you like a tool. Last but not least, your
mother. She was a casualty of ya stupidity! Weak mutha fuckas don't deserve to breathe!
All rats must die. I can't leave room for no mice!" Taking the Fisherman's hook knife

from out of his pocket! Kiem cut a thick slab of beef from a slaughtered cow, that hung close by. Then he took the knife and held its hook blade up in the air and came down with great pressure on Nicco's abdomen ripping it completely open all the way down to his naval. As blood gushed and squirted everywhere, his guts and intestines hung loose hanging out of his stomach. Shaking up on the hooks, Kiem already knew that he was gonna bleed out, but wanted this nigga to suffer! Removing the gag from his mouth Kiem stuffed the slab of beef into Nicco's mouth. Walking a few feet from where the bloodshed was enormous Kiem approached a steel cage and removed the black sheet from over it! Telling Don Smoke and Bandz to step out of the way, they both looked on with confusion as they heard the growls and panting of the unexpected! Kiem opened the lock then opened the door on the cage as two wolves ran out at full speed and attacked Nicco's body! Eating his guts like it was no other prey left in the world, one of the wolves jumped high and locked on to Nicco's face, ripping his mouth off with the slab of beef still in it! In shock Bandz couldn't move as Kiem picked her up and carried her outside! Quickly coming up out of her Tyvek suit, Bandz stood in front of Kiem and vomited all over him! "Damn Ma! You okay?" Kiem asked with deep concern. "Yea! Just give me a second." She replied while taking a few deep breaths. Kiem came up out of his Tyvek suit with the quickness, especially after Bandz spilled her gutz all over him. After gathering herself, Bandz opened Nicco's car door and hit the trunk button. "Jackpot!" She said out loud then quickly snatched up the duffle bag and tossed it into Kiem's back seat. "Let's get up outta here! We still got work to do!" Kiem stated. Bandz got in the car with Kiem and they pulled off heading to their next destination as Don Smoke followed. Making a run for the interstate, several fire trucks flew past them going in the opposite direction. They deep like shit, but ain't no ambulance with 'em! Something probably on fire somewhere! Kiem said to himself, not really caring too much!

Floating on the interstate Bandz came up out of her red bottoms and cat suit then quickly threw on a pair of jeans and t-shirt that she had in her bag before putting on her sneakers. Taking her chain and earrings off, she put them inside of Kiem's console then gave him a brief rundown. "We go in, snatch up the bitch, get the safe open, and we out! Anything interfere with what we came here for, we lay that shit and move out! This ain't one of them easy, slide in and out, we could've got rich type of jobs!" Bandz explained. "This bitch keepz a few shooters up in the spot. We don't want to alert their attention." Bandz explained. "Factz!!" Kiem stated. "Thatz why we handle the job with these!" Reaching back into her bag, she pulled out several silencers. "Okay! Now we a few points up in the game!"

Riding the side blocks of Jersey City, Bo$$ thought about heading back to the Brickz, but he wanted to find this purple Benz and handle shit. The arson job wasn't nothing. But if I can find this purple Benz and the bitch who owns it I can cash out big on top of what I already was paid. Continuing to take side blocks around the city, Bo$$ decided to pull over on Winfield Ave. as he drove down the dark street. Opening two bags of dope, he hit each bag with the quickness and slid back in the driver's seat, as he went into a nod.

Seeing the big bright letters "HT", which said "Hammer Time" underneath, as he drove by let Kiem know that this was a well-established joint. That sign alone had to cost about $250k. Kiem said to himself. Pulling off the interstate, Kiem circled the establishment looking for anything that resembled any ties or affiliation with Hammer Time. Circling the entire parking lot, Don Smoke circled it going in the opposite direction from Kiem. Meeting up in the middle of the parking lot they signaled to each other to park by the front entrance. With a total of four surveillance cameras, one on each corner of the building, the ghost was clear in the parking lot. This bitch have some wealthy customer's! So I know that safe is holding something nice! Kiem stated. I'm bankin' on it 2! Bandz said. Removing all his jewelry except for his pinky ring, Kiem placed it inside of his console. then touched his dash screen, as the back seat of the Panamera rotated revealing the Gold AR with the drums. "I know you ready! Where you get this pretty bitch from?" Bandz stated then asked. "It was a gift but no worries, we all getting new toys!" Kiem stated. Don Smoke opened his trunk and took out the duffle bags, then made his way to Kiem's car. They all strapped on a vest, then gloves, followed by their ski masks. Ready to go, the squad made a run for the front entrance. Bandz entered first and spotted the Chinese woman who had her back turned. As Kiem hopped over the desk and smacked the Chinese bitch with his Glock across the back of her head! Blood instantly started to flow, but it was too late for the woman to alert security as Kiem had his gun stuck all the way inside her mouth. "Shut the fuck up and don't try to say shit or ya ass will swallow these bullets! Do you understand me bitch?" Kiem harshly stated. Bandz zip tied her hands behind her back then told her to walk to the back office. The woman was resistant at first, 'til Bandz dumbed out on her right quick. "Bitch you think it's a game!" She stated coldly as she shot the woman in her shoulder. Kiem muzzled her mouth with his hand and dragged her into the back room with ease. "Now open da fuckin' safe if you want to live! You got exactly 2 minutes to open it!" Bandz demanded. Speaking in Chinese she kept going on, 'til Kiem punched her dead in the eye, knocking her to the floor. Lifting her back on her feet, he coldly stated. "Bitch listen! Either open this safe, or you die. Ya kids and ya family die too!" Shaking as she struggled to see the numbers on the safe dial, she started to enter the combination. Two tall white men entered the office through the side room door, and immediately reached for their weapons! Kiem quickly shot both men in the head! Brains splattered all over the wall. With the safe now open, Bandz hurried and filled up the duffle bags, one after the next! The Chinese woman stood there helpless and watched Bandz empty the safe. The four duffle bags were full, and then Kiem saw some manilla file folders up against the back of the safe wall. Grabbing the folders, he opened them up and noticed pictures of him at different locations doing a variety of things. Going through the folders they revealed pictures of him in the nude at his condo, pictures of him and Bliss in the shower, the bedroom, and on the living room floor of his condo making out. "Sick bitch!" He said out loud. "This bitch been watching me from the jump!" Kiem stated. Opening the last folder it revealed two pictures of Bliss, one with an big red x across the whole picture, then another one with the acronym "KOS" on the front. "Kill On Sight." Hearing footsteps approaching, he quickly tossed the folders into one of the duffle bags and stood behind the door! Three medium build men entered the room, and started speaking Russian, then pulled their weapons, soon as they witnessed the dead men on the floor. Kiem let the Tec spray watching as the men bodies jerked from the rapid gunfire! Getting up from behind the office desk, Bandz held the women at gunpoint then asked, "How many men are armed in here?" "A couple. It's more in the basement watching over the escorts. Then the rooms where the children work!" The Chinese woman stated. "What da fuck you mean rooms where the children work?" Bandz angrily asked. "The young girls that Ms. Estelvo purchases from different countries. She keeps them locked in luxury rooms in the basement lounge and makes them perform sexual acts with older men." The woman stated before Bandz pistol whipped the woman across her face, cussing her out in disgust. "You no good bitch! How dare you harm an innocent child? You deserve to die bitch! You hear me? You're gonna die bitch!" "Ma! We gotta go. We ain't got time to unlock those doors! Where's the surveillance footage at?" Kiem asked the woman as she laid on the floor sobbing. Continuing to sob, she ignored Kiem's question. Kiem then stated in a calm, but cold tone of voice "I'm not gone ask you again!" as he put his Glock to her head. She quickly got with the program and pointed to the painting on the wall. Kiem hurried and moved the picture, then ejected the disc from the DVR and put it inside of his vest. then ripped the whole brain from the shelf with the cables, and stuffed it into a duffle bag. Looking out the door entrance he signaled for Don. Don Smoke entered the back office and quickly snatched up two duffle bags and headed towards his car. Bandz snatched up a bag as Kiem shot the Chinese woman in the back of her head three times. Barely reaching the front door, multiple shots rang out as a dozen or more men rushed Kiem and Bandz, speaking in Russian and shooting! Don Smoke knew it was the opps because the squad had silencers on their weapons.

Hitting shit on site he saw Kiem and Bandz posted behind the front desk, letting their hammer's fly. Covering for Bandz, Don told her to come with the bag, as him and Kiem shielded her! Making her way out the door she tossed the duffle bag into Don's trunk with the other two bags. Shots sprayed everywhere as these Russian mutha fuckas kept coming! Running outta ammo as they emptied clip after clip, Kiem knew that he had to make it to the AR! "Don we gotta cover Bandz and let her take this last bag!" Kiem said. "Say less my nigga!" He replied while knocking shit off by the two's. "Ma! Once you get outside, start the car and get in the driver's seat, open the roof all the way! On the count of two!" Kiem stated. "One. Two." as him and Don Smoke raised up from behind the desk side by side, hitting everything coming at 'em! Bandz took off with the last bag and made it out to the car. After putting the bag in the trunk with the rest, she hurried to the Porsche, got behind the wheel, started her up and opened the panoramic roof top. Backing up towards the door, more men kept coming from a distance. "This shit is crazy! The more mutha fuckas that die, the more that come!" Kiem exclaimed. "My nigga! Go get in the car, go straight to New Castle! Me and Bandz will meet you there!" "Nigga! I ain't goin' nowhere, we leaving this mutha fucka together!" Don Smoke expressed. "We don't have much left. Go now or we both gone be done, my nigga! I got something for their ass, soon as you make it to ya car and bounce." Kiem said. Doing as Kiem asked of him, Don Smoke made it out, and went straight to his car. Starting the engine, he threw back! The nigga walked up to Bandz and asked. "What you just say?" "You heard me nigga! I know damn well ya ugly ass ain't deaf!" Bandz boldly stated. Embarrassed by his homeboys laughing at him, he punched Bandz in the face causing her to stumble. Spitting on the ground she laughed before pulling her Glock and shooting the nigga, 3 times in his stomach. "What the fuck?!" Kiem said. Another one of the niggaz was creeping towards Bandz as she had her back turned towards him, standing over the nigga who she just shot! Aiming his gun at her, Kiem instantly got out of his car and raced towards Bandz calling her name, as several shots were fired! Pop! pop. pop. pop! Jumping in front of her, he fell to her feet. . Hitting everyone out there, she saw Honcho hiding behind a parked car. As Kiem laid at her feet. coughing and spiting up thick traces of blood! Bandz screamed crazily, as she looked at the three bullet holes in his chest! "Hold on nigga. Don't fuckin' die on me! Please don't! Not today Kiem! Not today!" She sadly expressed. Seeing nothing but white clouds and bright lights everything flashed across his mind! All his childhood memories, the game that his brother Nice tried to keep him away from! The loyalty that he gave! The respect and love that he got from everyone! His right hand man Don Smoke coming home to a brand new Lexus! The day that him and Bliss made it official! The squad and all their epic moments! Yep! It was now time. Time to take that ride, time to finally close the chapter!

To be continued…